"Lock the door, Savannah,"
Mike said roughly.

She hurt for him. Whatever had happened that day had been bad. She ran her hand across the nape of his neck, his curls brushing her fingers like strands of silk.

He turned to look down at her, his eyes burning with need. As she reached for him, he crushed her to his lean body and kissed her as if it was the first kiss he'd been allowed in years. It was no lazy, teasing kiss, but a bruising, hungry longing that was fierce in its demand.

It took her breath away, set her aflame, made her want to yield to him and give until all his pain and need was gone. . . .

WHAT ARE *LOVESWEPT* ROMANCES?

They are stories of true romance and touching emotion. We believe those two very important ingredients are constants in our highly sensual and very believable stories in the *LOVESWEPT* line. Our goal is to give you, the reader, stories of consistently high quality that may sometimes make you laugh, sometimes make you cry, but are always fresh and creative and contain many delightful surprises within their pages.

Most romance fans read an enormous number of books. Those they truly love, they keep. Others may be traded with friends and soon forgotten. We hope that each *LOVESWEPT* romance will be a treasure—a "keeper." We will always try to publish

*LOVE STORIES YOU'LL NEVER FORGET
BY AUTHORS YOU'LL ALWAYS REMEMBER*

The Editors

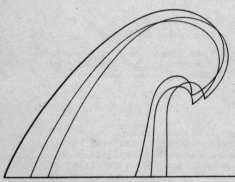

LOVESWEPT® • 195

Sara Orwig
Wind Warning

BANTAM BOOKS
TORONTO • NEW YORK • LONDON • SYDNEY • AUCKLAND

WIND WARNING

A Bantam Book / June 1987

LOVESWEPT® and the wave device are registered trademarks of Bantam Books, Inc. Registered in U.S. Patent and Trademark Office and elsewhere.

If you would be interested in receiving protective vinyl covers for your Loveswept books, please write to this address for information:

Loveswept
Bantam Books
P.O. Box 985
Hicksville, NY 11802

ISBN 0-553-21825-5

Published simultaneously in the United States and Canada

PRINTED IN THE UNITED STATES OF AMERICA

O   0 9 8 7 6 5 4 3 2 1

With thanks to Tim Orwig, Mary Orwig, Punch and Ann McBride, and George Orr, for answering questions.

One

It was the second week of June. A cabin cruiser, the *Marietta,* bobbed in the choppy green water of Lake Superior, while dark clouds began to spread across the northwestern horizon. Lightning zigzagged, and waves heightened beneath strong winds that whipped over the water's surface. Inside the stateroom of the *Marietta,* his feet propped on a settee, his long body stretched out in a chair, was Michael Jefferson Smith. Beneath a tangle of black curls, dark lashes were feathered on his cheeks. His broad chest rose and fell evenly as he dozed. The first big drops of rain tapped against the deck; then a sheet of rain swept over the cabin cruiser.

Lightning flickered and thunder rumbled, until one particular bolt crackled in the air and a clap of thunder banged like a gunshot. Mike opened his eyes and stared into space, momentarily befuddled. A wave crashed against the hull, and the *Marietta* tilted, pressing Mike against the side of the chair.

"Holy jeez," he muttered, realizing he was caught in a sudden storm. Galvanized into action, he rushed to the cockpit to start the engines. Swearing under his breath, he stared at blinding rain and a lake turned into a fury, waves indistinguishable from sheets of rain.

He couldn't make contact with the Coast Guard on the radio. Knowing he wasn't far from shore, cursing the fact that he had been asleep instead of monitoring Coast Guard storm warnings, he calculated the shortest distance to land and turned south, his dark brows drawing together in a frown of concentration. The sound of thunder was as constant as the crash of waves. The *Marietta* rocked and rose, to slam down with jarring force. Mike's pulse raced, and he swore another stream of oaths, this time directed at himself for having been born with the ability to sleep like a hibernating bear.

Suddenly, as the boat rose on the crest of a wave, he could see a structure looming ahead. For a ridiculous instant he thought it was a floating building. The dark, bulky object was dead ahead, and Mike leaned on the horn and turned the wheel, but it was too late to avoid a collision. He instantly realized he had miscalculated how close he was to shore, running in too fast and coming upon some structure that was built out over the water.

He abandoned the wheel and ran out on the bridge. As the deck tilted, he slipped, regained his balance, and skinned down the ladder to the deck. Lightning flashed, and for one second suspended in time, Mike saw a big, square, old-fashioned houseboat wallowing like an elephant in the water, and he saw a thin guy run out of the cockpit.

For a chilling moment Mike thought *they* had found him, remembering the last attempt on his life. Then the thought was gone, as space between the boats vanished.

The *Marietta* tilted again. Mike slid, pushed away, and jumped for his life. The first splintering jar came as he left the boat and plunged into the cold water.

When he broke the surface he flailed his arms, fighting to survive. Ahead was the solid bulk of the houseboat, and he tried to swim for it. The lake tossed him around, washing him back and defeating his efforts. As a wave caught him and he fought for his life, struggling against the forces of the storm and lake, he glimpsed the *Marietta* slipping beneath the churning water. His mind went blank to everything except survival, and he thrashed until he couldn't last any longer. His fingers touched something solid.

With a groan he struggled to get a handhold.

His fingers closed on wood and he clung, too exhausted to try to pull himself out of the water. Hands grasped his arms and tugged.

Realizing help and safety had come, he made a supreme effort. He pulled until his muscles felt as if they would pop. He scraped his torso on the deck of the houseboat as he came half out of the water. The exertion took his last bit of energy. Blackness enveloped him and he lost consciousness.

Savannah Carson heaved the man up onto the deck, tugging his legs out of the water. She straddled him, pushing on his back, trying to rid his lungs of water. Her heart thudded wildly in fear, and she rolled him over, moving above him as she tried to remember her CPR training. She had been so frightened by the storm that she'd gone out on deck to check if the boat was secured, and had discovered the *Bluebell* had broken its moorings and drifted away from shore. Then she had wasted precious time trying to start the motor.

The storm had caught her in all its fury, and her worries had grown to enormous proportions as the *Bluebell* floundered in rough water. Her fear had heightened to thought-stopping terror when she glimpsed the cabin cruiser coming straight toward the houseboat. Panicking at the last minute, she had run outside to shout, and then the crash had knocked her off her feet. She saw a man dive from the oncoming boat, and she had gone through agony until she spotted him bobbing in the water near the houseboat.

In desperation she tried to throw him a line, but he wouldn't grasp it. Finally his hands had closed on the deck of the houseboat, and she had hauled him on board. She was drenched to the skin, chilled to the bone, and terrified the man might not survive. She tilted his head back, opened his mouth, and bent over him.

"Please," she whispered, "please come around. Say something. . . ." she urged, looking down at features that stirred a new kind of fear within her. He had dark lashes, bronzed skin, and black hair, which was plastered to his head. But his prominent cheekbones, his slightly crooked nose, the white scar that ran across his temple and the other along his jaw, gave him a harsh, rugged appearance that disturbed her. His lashes fluttered, and for a second, dazed blue eyes looked up at her.

Suddenly he bucked and came up with a roar. She saw his fist and jerked her head away, catching a glancing blow on her jaw. At the same time the blow struck her, he heaved her away, and she slid across the deck, crashing into a chair. Dimly she thought that people do see stars when they've been hit. She shook her head. Her jaw felt broken. Breathless with panic, forgetting the jarring pain, she watched as the man got to his feet and started toward her, rage evident in his eyes.

Wondering what kind of madman she had collided with and fished out of the lake, she scrambled up and snatched the first weapon she could find, an ax, which was secured to the bulkhead.

With a yell she held it back over her shoulder like a baseball bat, and he stopped in his tracks.

As the *Bluebell* rolled and bobbed in the rough water, and wind and rain whipped across the decks, Savannah braced her hip against the bulkhead, trying to keep her balance, ready for an attack.

The man she faced wore a T-shirt that molded strong muscles, the scars on his face gave him a threatening air, and the fury in his blue eyes took her breath away. She watched him crouch and double his fists, and she gripped the ax tightly, scared she wouldn't stand a chance against the stranger's strength.

Groggy from his ordeal, Mike wavered on his feet, shock sending a momentary rush of adrenaline pumping through him, giving him a bit of renewed energy. Furious over the sunken *Marietta*, nerves on edge from his situation, he reacted with anger. Only feet away, threatening him with an ax, stood a slender adversary. But rain had drenched the person's clothing, and it molded to a body that was absolutely and unmistakably a woman's! Mike's fear that someone had deliberately rammed his boat and intended to finish him off vanished as he stared at her. Her hair hung in wet strands down her back, most of it hidden by a soggy sailor cap that looked like a melted mushroom on her head.

"You're a woman!" he snapped, more to himself than her, aghast that he had actually struck her.

"You come one step closer," she shouted, trying to make herself heard above the storm's roar, "and I'll ax you!" She was shaking so violently, she could barely stand.

"Hey! I thought you were a guy," Mike said, acutely aware that her lip was bleeding and that he had socked a woman. "I'm sorry. I thought you were a man. This damned tub—it looks like the ark—ran me down!"

"Your boat hit mine! Stay where you are!" She backed up a step as he moved forward a step. He made a move toward her, and she raised the ax higher, ready to swing.

"Will you put the ax down? I wouldn't have hit you if I'd known you were a woman."

She glared at him in disbelief, while Mike stood with his hand on a lifeline and stared back at her.

Soggy, bedraggled, bristling, with the ax poised, she looked as if someone had fished *her* out of the lake. He could have taken the ax from her in seconds, but he didn't want to hurt her again or alarm her. "We can't stand here much longer without being washed over the side. Can we go inside to discuss this?" he shouted.

Savannah stood still in indecision for only a second. Then she lowered the ax. "You go first."

Still wary, her knees shaking in an aftermath of reaction, she struggled across the deck after him. The wind had abated slightly, making walking less hazardous, but the rain came straight down in a cold, steady deluge. The cheerful yellow striped awning that covered one side of the houseboat had been ripped away by the wind. Only a tattered triangle was left hanging near the door. She followed the stranger inside, then slammed the door shut and raised the ax again.

"Put the ax down! I'm sorry I hit you. I didn't know you were a woman," he said again.

She wasn't sure his speech reassured her or made her feel any better, but she lowered the ax even though she believed she was facing a criminal. He looked every inch the movie stereotype of a mobster. "Who are you?"

"I'm . . ." There was a fraction of a moment's pause while he made a split-second decision to hide his true identity, as he had promised to do. Caution warned him to use another name until he knew more about the woman. "Miles Seth," he finished.

"I'm Savannah Carson," she said, wondering if he had paused because he was making up a name.

They stood staring at each other in silence. "You sank my boat," he said accusingly.

"You ran into me!" she snapped, her eyes flashing fire.

"Yeah, well, we can discuss that later. Will you put away that ax? I'm harmless."

He looked anything but harmless. As she took a deep breath, she tried to decide whether or not to trust him.

With her audible intake of breath Mike wondered why he had ever held the notion she was a man. As she breathed deeply, the white T-shirt molded like skin to her body, revealing upthrusting breasts above a tiny waist. He couldn't keep from staring. She was beautifully shaped, and might as well have been nude. Then he saw her reaction. Her nipples hardened, and he felt a stir of desire. Finally looking up, he saw her cheeks had reddened too. With big green eyes and a figure that turned heads, she was causing something to awaken within him. He tried to look elsewhere and change his thoughts. Glancing at the ax, he remembered the sunken boat and his dilemma, and ardor cooled like rain on the deck. He spotted a box of tissues nearby, pulled one out, and turned to approach her, ready to act if she swung the ax.

"Your mouth is bleeding," he said, looking into her wide eyes. He had to admire her courage in confronting him, and he hated to his bones the fact that he had hit her. "Stand still."

Savannah felt rooted to the spot, but her emotions were doing somersaults. He was close, only inches away. His voice was deep, resonant, and more warming than a fire. His blue eyes were direct, and the smoldering look he had given her wet T-shirt had done things to her system that were more intense than the storm. His command to stand still had been gentle, his apology had sounded sincere, and his voice had been pure magic. Fear and anger dissipated like wind-blown fog, replaced by curiosity and attraction. If he intended to hit her again, she might just let him!

He tilted her chin up to dab gently at the cut at the corner of her mouth. His fingers were warm and firm on her chin, and she was aware of his touch to the last little dusty corner of her brain. And she was equally conscious of the close scrutiny he was giving her mouth.

Suddenly his eyes twinkled. "Do you always take an ax to battle when you're threatened?"

She gave him a lopsided smile. "This is a first in my life."

"It's an unforgettable first for me too." He winked at her. "I hope we have more firsts—all good ones, of course." He dabbed gently at her mouth. "I really am sorry," he said, his voice dropping a notch lower and stirring her pulse. "But then, you sank my boat," he added gently.

"I told you, I didn't mean to, and you did it yourself—you ran into me," she said persistently, remembering her panic when she had spotted his boat heading straight for hers.

"What's this tub doing out on the lake in a storm?" He lifted the soggy sailor cap off her head and tossed it to a chair, where it landed with a plop. If he liked her better without the cap, he didn't give any indication, but she became miserably aware of her bedraggled appearance. He moved a few inches closer, and suddenly the chill she had felt diminished, changing to heat.

"Kindly stop calling it a tub," she said softly, thinking more about him than the *Bluebell*. "The houseboat drifted away from the bank. I don't know what happened to the ropes, but when I realized I was drifting, I tried to start the motor. I don't know how—"

"You don't know how?" he interrupted, his voice losing its inviting tone.

"No," she said, her cheeks growing warm. "I guess I should have learned."

"I would think so. Damn," he said, his charm disappearing. "I've never known anyone who owned a boat and didn't know how to run the engine!" He handed her the tissue and moved away a fraction, his voice becoming brisk with annoyance. "All you have to do is turn a key!"

"I know that much," she said coolly. "I tried to turn it, and—"

"You should—"

"If you'll let me finish," she said in a low voice, trying to control her impatience. "I don't know anything about boats except that they float. I don't own this houseboat. It's my sister and her husband's, and they told me to come stay for a couple of weeks and relax. The boat is never away from the shore. I don't know how it came loose from the dock, but it did, for the first time since I've ever been on it. I turned the key and the motor wouldn't kick over."

He grinned at her. Like a flash of lightning, his grin transformed the surroundings, and she felt better instantly.

"That's a pretty good reason. I guess I was a little hasty in my judgment."

"Apology accepted. The generator works, thank goodness, so we have electricity."

"I think the first order of the day is for me to go to the cockpit and try to start the motor. We need some power before this thing fills with water and goes down like my boat. Did you turn on the bilge pump?"

"Yes, I did."

"Good for you. Is it an outboard or inboard motor?"

"Inboard." Waggling her head at him, she laughed. "You know, you have to face the fact that you ran into me. Head-on. If I hadn't grabbed a lifeline, I would have been tossed overboard by the impact. I didn't hit you!"

He grinned again. "We'll settle that issue when we call the insurance companies, okay? Let me try the motor."

She led the way, and stood shivering, hugging her arms around her waist, as she watched him. He turned the key, and they heard a grinding sound. After several more tries he swore softly under his breath. Savannah experienced a mixture of feelings—worry over having no way to control the houseboat, and satisfaction that she hadn't failed because of incompetence.

"Before I go to the engine compartment to look for the trouble, let's dry off. Does your brother-in-law have any clothes on board?"

"Yes. There are two staterooms—here, I'll show you."

She led him to the stateroom where Paris and Van kept their things. She fished out a pair of dry jeans and a clean plaid shirt, then rummaged for a pair of shorts and some socks. "You can sleep in here. I'm staying in the forward stateroom. Here are some old sneakers, but I think your feet are bigger than Van's."

Mike smiled as he took the dry clothing, his fingers brushing hers lightly. She was acutely aware of the warmth of his hands. "This'll do. Better than being wet. Get going and change. You feel like ice."

Her teeth were almost chattering with the cold. She rushed out of the stateroom, then remembered the towels. "Mr. Seth, the towels are in this cabinet," she said, waving her hand to indicate the closet behind her.

"What? Oh, yeah, thanks."

She left the room, puzzled because she could have sworn he hadn't recognized his own name for a second. Deciding that the thought was ridiculous and feeling more and more aware of the current of attraction that flared between them, she rushed to the smaller, forward stateroom. It served as a bedroom for her two nephews most of the time, but was her room now. She enjoyed the novelty of being surrounded by the boys' toys, and the room always seemed cheerful to her.

She dried herself and changed quickly, bracing her hip against the bulkhead to keep from losing her balance as the wind and rough water buffeted the houseboat. She wondered how they would work out paying for the damage to the houseboat and Miles Seth's sunken boat. Miles Seth was an unusual name. And he was an unusual man. She touched her bruised jaw lightly. He had seemed truly apologetic, but there had been no mistaking the toughness in him during their initial confrontation.

After drying her hair and letting it fall freely over her shoulders, she dressed in jeans and a red sweat shirt, then returned to the salon to peer out the portholes. They were being drenched with rain.

Mike was already in the salon. She didn't notice him, and he took the opportunity to stare at her. Her golden hair fell to the middle of her back, straight and shiny, looking like spun silk, and he wanted to run his fingers over it. She had evoked a contradictory mixture of emotions in him since the first moment he had glimpsed her, waving at him before he had jumped into the lake. "Hasn't let up much, has it?" he said.

She turned, her green eyes wide. Her lip was still swollen, and there was a faint bluish tint to her jaw. He saw her bite back a laugh and remembered his appearance. Grinning, he held out his hands. "I'm a little taller than your brother-in-law."

Savannah fought to stifle a laugh. The jeans were too short, too loose on his narrow hips, and were gathered in puckers beneath his own belt. The sleeves of the blue-and-gray plaid shirt were rolled to his elbows, and the too-small shirt pulled tautly across his broad shoulders. With his hair dry now, she noticed it was thick and curly and slightly streaked with gray. He looked as dangerous as ever, but twice as handsome. Even the ill-fitting clothes couldn't hide the aura he possessed of a sensual, self-assured male.

"The jeans barely fit," he said dryly, patting his hip. "But they're better than wet clothes."

Suddenly they felt a jarring slam as the houseboat struck something. A scraping noise followed, and Savannah was thrown off her feet, falling forward toward Mike.

Two

Mike's strong arms closed around Savannah's waist to catch her, and they both toppled, hitting the side of a chair and falling to the deck. Pain exploded in her shoulder, and she yelped. Breath was forced from her lungs as he rolled on top of her. She felt his hard body, his legs tangling with hers, as she lay beneath him. Mike caught a whiff of a delicious scent of lilies and apple blossoms, and unconsciously tightened his arms a fraction, relishing the feel of her soft body pressed against him, feeling a swift arousal.

"Are you hurt?" he asked with concern, his face inches above hers. For a second Savannah's pain was obliterated and her only awareness was of the man lying on top of her.

"No," she whispered. His eyes narrowed, his gaze lowering to her mouth, and Savannah felt a burst of desire deep inside her. Aware that he was a stranger, feeling as if she had slipped and fallen into a hot fire, she tried to wriggle free. "Will you move!"

He flashed a knowing grin and stood up, then reached down to help her to her feet. She came up to stand in a narrow space between a chair, the bulkhead, and Mike. "Are you okay?" he asked.

"I bumped my shoulder. I'm okay." *Or I would be if you'd move,* she wanted to add. His blue eyes were thickly lashed, and seemed to capture her gaze and hold it. If he heard her, he gave no indication, but stared at her intently. She felt ensnared in invisible bonds. Her gaze lowered to his lips. They were well shaped, the underlip full, sensual. She tilted her head to one side in a quizzical manner, and his brows arched.

"You're wondering the same thing I am," he drawled, his words as sensuous as his tone.

It took a second for what he had said to register. When it did, her gaze flew up to meet his, and she blushed.

Amusement and a look of satisfaction flared in his eyes. "Son of a gun, Savannah, you *were* wondering the same thing!"

"How do you know?" she asked, her voice slightly breathless. "I'm wondering what's happened to the boat."

His mocking grin told her how much he believed her. "You probably ran down a second boat."

"Will you move out of the way so we can go look!"

"You stay inside." He smiled and touched her arm. "Is there a jacket around?"

"Yes," she said. She squeezed past him to get a poplin jacket, wondering why he had such a devastating effect on her.

He headed for the door, and in a few long strides was gone. She was about to follow him when he jumped back inside and slammed the door. "We've hit shore, thank heavens! I want to secure the boat, if you'll give me some line. Now that we're aground, I'll wait until tomorrow before I tackle trying to fix the motor."

"I'll help you tie us down."

"Stay inside and keep dry and warm," he urged, catching her wrist. His touch sent a current zinging between them, and again she became aware of Miles Seth as a man. Her gaze dropped to his mouth, and a fleeting curiosity rushed through her mind as she wondered what it would feel like to have his lips pressed against hers.

"Where's some line?" he asked softly, looking suddenly amused.

Startled over the way she had been staring, and mildly embarrassed, as she feared he had guessed her thoughts a second time, she turned to get the line.

In minutes they were outside. Cold rain lashed at them, and to Savannah's relief she saw that the houseboat had run aground on a spot of sloping shoreline. Pine trees were only dark blurs through the steady rain, but they looked solid and secure. With a coil of line over his shoulder, Mike scrambled out onto the bow. He found a frayed bit of line trailing in the water and realized the worn threads were probably the reason the *Bluebell* had drifted away from shore. He shook his head at the carelessness of Savannah and her relatives as he tied the frayed line around the base of the closest tree. He glanced up to see Savannah working to fasten another line to a tree.

For an instant he thought of his precarious position. He didn't want to draw attention to himself, yet here he was caught in a storm with a stranger on a runaway houseboat, stranded somewhere along the vast shoreline of Lake Superior. For a moment he looked over his shoulder at the rugged, tree-covered slope behind him. He could just disappear—but would he be any safer? As swiftly as the notion had come, he rejected it, because he had no idea of his location. He would still be at the mercy of strangers—strangers who weren't one ninety-ninth as attractive as the exciting woman he'd just met!

Did Savannah have a family who would stir up a fuss searching for her? He decided he'd better stick to the name Miles Seth, because he didn't know anything about her; whom she was related to, her contacts. But deception was something new and repugnant to him. Particularly if it wasn't necessary. And, he had to admit, particularly with Savannah. He had been drawn to her from the moment she had faced him, ready to defend herself. He hoped he could learn enough about her to tell her the truth soon. Realizing he was getting soaked, he uncoiled the line on his shoulder.

Savannah finished a knot, relieved to be anchored again and out of imminent danger. She looked at the tough stranger working near her. He was hunkered down, tugging on a line, his jeans pulling tautly over his knees and muscular thighs. He finished and jumped back onto the houseboat with agility. What was it about him that made her so self-conscious and so conscious of him? she wondered. She felt young again when he looked at her with his bedroom blue eyes, but she didn't understand her reaction. They hardly knew each other. With her ex-husband, Tyler, there had been a long, growing mutual attraction—not something that had burst between them like spontaneous combustion!

Savannah caught a brief look from Miles Seth that stirred sparks as surely as if he had touched her. She smiled and hurried back to the houseboat.

Inside they shook off their wet jackets. "Now that the boat is stable enough, I can cook," she said. "Want hot chocolate or coffee?"

"Hot chocolate," he answered, thinking a nice dollop of bourbon might be better. For the first time

Mike paused to take in his surroundings. Papers were strewn everywhere, and books were scattered around, probably having tumbled off furniture in the storm. Toys had spilled from a box. Pillows had fallen off chairs, plants had tipped and spilled dirt, all clear indications to Mike that the houseboat hadn't been intended for sailing out on the lake, but probably had been permanently anchored at the dock. The place was comfy, cluttered, and old. For an instant he thought of the sleek, well-equipped yacht, now at the bottom of Lake Superior. Even though it wasn't his yacht, the *Marietta* had been loaned to him for his own use, and it was new, plush, and comfortable. Neat. This was a floating tub filled with junk. He sighed, knowing when he had hauled himself over the side, it had seemed like Paradise.

Savannah was bending over looking into the refrigerator. Jeans molded to her well-rounded bottom, and her golden hair dangled past her shoulders. She straightened and gave a flick of her head, sending her hair flying in a cascade of gold, while she slanted him a look. He felt a jump in his pulse and moved closer to lean his hip against a counter. "Are you married, Miss Carson?"

"Nope, and you can call me Savannah."

"And you can call me Miles." This time he remembered. Miles Seth. He had better remember. "Do you work?"

As she smiled, her full red lips parted, a dimple appeared in her cheek, and her green eyes flashed. He moved a few inches closer. She was a knockout. Single, but there had to be a man. He glanced down and saw the plain gold band and the large diamond on her finger.

"I'm a teacher," she answered as she turned to the stove.

"You were married."

Again she slanted him a look. There were moments when her green eyes were like a cat's. "Yes, but I've been divorced for quite a few years."

He chuckled, and her brows arched quizzically. "Quite a few years," he said mockingly. "You're too young to have been divorced quite a few years."

She smiled again, the adorable dimple in her cheek reappearing. She sparkled when she smiled, and he forgot the storm, the sunken yacht, danger, the lies about his identity. He forgot everything except Mrs. Savannah Carson.

"Hardly too young," she said, "but thanks. I'm thirty-six."

Pleasantly surprised, Mike inched a little closer without conscious thought of what he was doing. "That's nice," he said, mentally calculating that if he'd had to guess at her age, he would have estimated her to be a full eight years younger. Maybe it was her long, blond hair or her wide green eyes that gave her a younger appearance. But thirty-six was nice. Very nice.

"Speak for yourself," she said with another heartwarming smile, as she set a skillet on the stove. "I'm famished. I haven't eaten a bite all day, including breakfast. Can you eat a hamburger?"

"Of course. Let me do the honors," he said, turning to wash his hands. As they worked together, she making a salad, he cooking the hamburgers, his curiosity about her grew. "What age kids do you teach?"

"I teach remedial reading in high school. I just got out for the summer. That's why I have some free time to stay on the houseboat. What do you do?"

He should have thought ahead! he realized. He hadn't considered at all what questions he might have to answer. "I'm an . . . accountant with the Acme Company."

"Where's the Acme Company located?" she asked.

He thought "Acme Company" sounded phony, and wished he had gotten his act together sooner. "In Duluth," he said, trying to stick as close to the truth as possible, yet at the same time feverishly trying to memorize each fact he was telling her. She turned and looked at him in surprise, and he held his breath, afraid she had discovered some flaw in his answer.

"I live in Duluth!"

He let out his breath, relieved that was all she had intended to say. Yet now he faced new worries. She should have read about him in the papers. As quickly as the thought came, he realized she would have read about Michael Smith, not Miles Seth, and he relaxed again. Then another worry surfaced. Her ties were in Duluth. It would be easy for her to let word out about him, accidentally or deliberately.

As he mulled the problems over in his mind, he and Savannah compared neighborhoods, discovering they didn't live too far apart in a suburban area outside of Duluth, and he began to get nervous about her questions.

"What were you doing out on the lake in the storm?" she asked, pausing as she carried dishes to the table.

"Fishing," he said, able to answer halfway truthfully. He took a deep breath of her perfume as she passed him. "I went below and fell asleep, and when I sleep I'm unconscious." He grinned. "I slept through the wind warnings."

Gazing into his sexy eyes, Savannah felt as if she were sleeping through a wind warning of her own.

"I woke up in the wind and rain and tried to run for shore," he finished.

"Do you know where we are?"

"Nope. This is my first time on this lake."

Disappointment showed clearly on her features. "I've tried and tried to call for help, but the radio won't work. I hope we can get through to someone soon."

Mike hoped just the opposite, except he needed to get in touch with Fitzgerald, his lawyer. The burgers smelled delicious, and the cabin was cozy, now that the boat was anchored; rain drummed overhead, and Mike was with a beautiful, exciting woman. Suddenly he felt better than he had for weeks. For an instant he was tempted to tell Savannah the truth about himself. Then his cautious nature squelched the notion.

After a couple of bites of hamburger, she tilted her head to one side. "Are you married?" she asked, not realizing she was holding her breath.

"Nope. I'm a widower."

"I'm sorry. Any children?"

"Yes. Brian. He's at a summer session of Semester-at-Sea, and probably halfway around the world right now." Her eyes widened, and she tilted her head to look at Mike with such obvious curiosity that he laughed.

"What happened? My nose turn blue?"

"No, but you have a son in college?"

His grin widened. "Yes, ma'am. And I get bills regularly to prove it. There's plenty of gray up here," he said, pointing to his hair. "I'm forty-two."

"That's great," she said, not realizing until the words were out how pleased she sounded. She stared at him, her hamburger forgotten.

"I'm glad you like my age so much." He was unable to resist the temptation to touch her, thinking she made him feel younger, more alive. He placed his knuckles beneath her chin. "How's your mouth?"

"Sore," she answered truthfully.

He touched the other corner of her mouth, and

sparks sizzled as she gazed steadily into his eyes. "What a shame. I'm sorry."

She wanted to smile and wave her hand casually and tell him to forget it, but she couldn't say a word. His finger traced tiny, searing circles at the corner of her mouth. Her breath caught in her throat, and she couldn't keep her lips closed. She reached up to make him stop, closing her hand around his wrist, but instead of stopping him she was like Brer Rabbit ensnared twice as strongly when he pushed on the Tar Baby.

"We hardly know each other," she finally whispered.

"We'll remedy that—fast!"

"Miles . . ."

She saw something suddenly flicker in his eyes—distaste, anger, guilt—as if he didn't like being addressed by his name. There was only one reason being called Miles should bother him—it wasn't his real name! She released his wrist and leaned back, the spell broken as she remembered how little she knew about him, how much she was taking for granted.

Glancing around, he waved his hand. "You read a lot?"

"Yes, I love to read," she said, wondering if she had imagined his reaction. He seemed completely at ease now. It had been the barest flicker in his eyes. Perhaps it had been nothing. She looked at his scars and was curious about what had happened to him, but was too polite to ask. "I'm working on some programs to use next year at school. The storm has shuffled everything."

"I can help you sort it out."

"Thanks. I accept your offer."

He put his hand on his chin and leaned closer to her again, the need to reach out and touch her growing more compelling. She reminded him of an enticing, sun-drenched meadow; inviting, warm, and fascinating.

"You don't look like a teacher."

She didn't want to tell him what she thought he looked like. "Oh? How do I look?"

He leaned even closer to her, and said, "You look gorgeous." He let his voice deepen, drawing out the words to see if he could elicit another response from her. "Green eyes like crystals—"

Savannah felt as if she were on fire. The man could turn on sensual charm like music on a radio. "That wasn't what I meant!" she said, trying to smile and be casual. "What sort of profession suits me?"

"Ah, that's easy too. Model, actress—"

She laughed, and his eyes twinkled with pleasure. "You're not too far off base. I majored in fashion merchandising and was a buyer in a store and occasionally did local modeling."

"And you went from that to teaching?" he asked, a note of incredulity in his voice.

"Teaching is satisfying," she said lightly, and he had a feeling she had more of a reason for changing professions than she was indicating. "What do we do about your boat?"

"We can't fish it from the bottom of the lake," he said, grinning.

"No, I mean do we have to contact the Coast Guard as well as the insurance companies? I'll have to tell my brother-in-law that you did hit me."

"As lovely and charming as you are, we may have to go ten rounds on that one. You hit me."

She firmed her lips, raised her chin, and shook her head, making her long hair shimmer in the light, and he knew he had a fight on his hands. For an instant he remembered the moment she had confronted him with the ax, and he laughed. "Don't get your ax."

"I won't get the ax. But to my last breath I will declare the truth—you ran right into me. I'll bet the houseboat has a chunk knocked out of it!"

"Who would know with this tub!" He waved his hand at her. "This floating mountain rammed me head on!"

She shook her head stubbornly, and he was amused. She was too beautiful and interesting to stir his anger. "Savannah." He drew out the word, and there was a flicker of response in her eyes. The stubborn lift to her chin vanished and her lips parted as she breathed deeply. He realized what a sensuous woman she was when she responded to something as mild as the sexy drawl of her name. His interest in her deepened. "I like your name. Are you from the South?"

"No, Mom just liked the name. My sisters are named Virginia, Brittany, and Paris. They're called Ginny, Brit, and Paris."

"I like the choices." He glanced down at his plate, then at hers. "You said you were hungry—we've let the burgers get as cold as the lake."

She smiled, her eyes sparkling. "I guess I forgot about hunger."

"That does it." He stood up. "We'll clean the galley later. Come in here. I have to fix something."

He took her arm as they entered the salon. Mike looked at the clutter of papers on every available surface. He picked a spot on the built-in sofa and nudged some papers to the floor to give them just enough room to sit close together.

"What are you going to fix?" she asked, laughter in her voice.

He turned her and sat her down, then plunked himself next to her, letting his arm rest behind her over the back of the yellow vinyl sofa. "I'm going to fix the fact that we're strangers. We're going to get to know each other."

She laughed, amused and intrigued, deciding she had imagined his reaction to his name. He was sexy and charming, and she was absolutely agreeable to the idea of getting to know him better. He caught a strand of her hair, toying with it as he asked, "What do you plan to do with the rest of your summer?"

"Mostly vacation. Get some projects ready for school. Maybe I'll do some part-time work as a sales clerk at DeVandever, the store where I used to be a buyer. I work there on holidays; they know me, and I know the store. It brings in a little extra income."

His voice dropped a notch. "Who's the man in your life?"

"Right now there isn't anyone I'm serious about. Just friends I date."

"Somehow I find it hard to believe they're just friends, but I'm enormously glad," he said truthfully.

"Who's the woman in your life?" she asked, arching an eyebrow, her eyes twinkling with a mixture of amusement and curiosity.

He shook his head. "None. Absolutely none. And if there were, I can't remember their names."

She laughed and he smiled, feeling delighted with her quicksilver laughter. His finger drifted across her cheek. "I'll be glad when your injuries are gone. I hate having hurt you, but I glimpsed you out in the rain flailing your arms, and the cap hid your hair and the rain hid your—"

"I'm sure it did," she said smartly.

He grinned and inched a fraction closer, dropping his gaze to her mouth. "How badly does it hurt?"

"I'm okay, really. Stop worrying about my mouth."

"You don't want me to kiss it and make it well?" he drawled softly, his gaze locking on hers with startling intensity.

She drew a deep breath. Without waiting for her answer, his attention shifted to her mouth again. Savannah's heart raced as he leaned closer, thudding so loudly, she thought he could hear it. She couldn't keep her eyes open. Her mouth tingled, and it wasn't from her injury. She wanted his kiss with a fierce compulsion. His lips brushed the corner of her mouth where she hadn't been hurt. It was a soft touch, like a thistle floating on the wind. Then she felt an explosion of fireworks inside. She curled her arms around his neck, conscious of the breadth of his shoulders and the faint, pleasant scent of his clothing and body. His knees pressed hers. He gently opened her mouth with his and took possession. She returned his kiss, aware of mild discomfort from her bruised lips, aware that he was trying to kiss her lightly.

His hands moved her, shifting her to his lap and cradling her head against his shoulder as he leaned over her. She slipped her hands across his shoulders, his neck, learning textures, weaving soft curls through her fingers. Finally she pushed away slightly. He paused, looking down at her with a dazed expression. "You make me feel alive again," he whispered, and she felt her heart lurch.

"We're going too fast," she whispered, making no effort to move out of the circle of his arms. He was so damned appealing! The scars and the crook in his nose gave him a ruthless air, but they weren't detracting, and they were offset quickly by his smiles and his personality. She ran her finger along his jaw and he closed his eyes, turning his head to kiss her hand, causing her pulse and breathing to flutter.

Knowing they were going too quickly, too intensely, she sat up and moved away. "I think we should go back to getting to know each other—in some way other than physically."

He smiled. "We can try," he said, but his words were husky and shaky, and she felt another catch in her breathing. He had the most profound effect on her, and she could tell from his actions that she had had an effect on him! She got up and moved away from him, knowing she would be back in his arms if she didn't.

"Maybe I should pick up my papers now," she said.

"Sure. Tell me how to help."

They worked together for the next hour, talking and laughing more than they sorted papers.

Finally Mike stood up reluctantly. "You sort your papers. I'll clean the galley."

"I'll help," she said, standing quickly. He leaned close, and they brushed against each other, shoulder to shoulder and hip to hip. She drew in her breath swiftly, conscious of the slightest contact between them.

"That's why you have to sort papers," he said with a mocking smile. He lowered his voice, seeing her green eyes darken. "We don't work together too well . . ." He slowed his words to see how much response he could get. "Because when we're together, we don't work."

"I suppose you're right," she whispered, her voice becoming throaty, fanning a warmth inside him.

He rested his hands on her shoulders. "I've never been attracted like this," he said "Leah, my wife, and I dated all through our senior year in high school and through college, until we married."

"I guess you should work in the galley," she said, changing the subject. She felt as if she had been caught in a whirlwind.

He smiled and left her, moving with a jaunty step. When he finished in the galley, she knew he was watching her even before she turned to meet his gaze.

"I'm going to shower and turn in," he said, and she nodded. She continued to stack papers, trying to straighten some of the clutter. After a few minutes she realized she hadn't changed the sheets in his stateroom. Hearing the shower running, she went to a cabinet to get out a set of clean sheets and then walked into his room. She stripped the bed, tossing the sheets into a heap. After putting on a fitted sheet, she quickly flipped open the clean top sheet, sending a card flying to the floor from the built-in shelves at the head of the bunk.

Savannah tucked in the sheet and went to pick up the card. It read, "Fitzgerald Tarkington," and gave a phone number but nothing else. She turned it over, thinking it was an odd calling card. If you didn't want anyone to know who you were, where you lived, or what business you were in, why would you have a calling card? She placed it on the shelf and saw Mike's billfold there, lying open. She didn't have to touch it to see the driver's license, which was tucked into one of the plastic holders. She leaned closer. *Michael Smith.* The name blinked at her as if it were in neon letters. The face was familiar but the name wasn't Miles Seth. And she realized her imagination hadn't played tricks on her when she had guessed earlier that he was using a false name.

She turned to stare at the door while her emotions churned. Though mildly angered and curious, she felt far more disappointment. As she wondered about Mr. Michael Smith, she remembered reading something in the *News Tribune and Herald* the day before about a bank robbery in Duluth, and there had been a description of the bank robber—white male, over six feet tall, dressed well in a suit . . . scars.

Savannah's lips firmed. She dropped the pillow in the middle of the bed and hurried to the salon to search for the paper. If Michael Smith were a bank robber, could she bear to reveal his identity to the authorities? Was she safe with him? Or was he a charming rogue who had been trying to lull her into trusting him for nefarious purposes? She couldn't believe he would harm her, but her fingers drifted lightly to her bruised jaw. How accidental had the blow been?

The newspaper she wanted wasn't in the stacks of papers and magazines she looked through. Then she remembered that she might have used it to line the trash basket. She picked up another paper and went to the galley. After laying the paper on the floor, she carefully lifted out the trash and dumped it onto the paper. Then she took the soiled paper out of the can, spread it out, and got down on her hands and knees. She brushed wet coffee grounds aside and saw it was the newspaper she had been searching for. Moving onion peel and more coffee grounds out of the way, she scanned the page to find the article she wanted.

"Robber Eludes Police," she read swiftly. "The Trinity Bank of Duluth—"

"Lose something?"

Three

Savannah's heart jumped. She looked up and saw Michael Smith standing in the doorway. His hair was damp, and the ends curled over his forehead. He'd dried his own clothes and was dressed in his jeans, but that was all. For a moment she was ensnared by a magnetic pull she couldn't resist as she looked at a bronzed, muscled chest covered by a triangle of curly dark hair. The triangle tapered to a thin line and disappeared beneath his low-slung, faded jeans, and she noticed another scar across his shoulders. That reminded her of his deception.

"Oh, no! I was reading something," she said, at a loss for a reasonable answer.

A slow, curious grin tugged at the corners of his mouth, and she scrambled to her feet.

"Aren't you a little desperate for news?" he asked, laughing. "You like reading through coffee grounds?"

As she reached down to scoop up the paper, tanned fingers closed around her wrist and stopped her. Her head jerked up, and she saw his curious, alert eyes look at her intently, then shift to the food-strewn paper.

She looked down. The bank-robbery article was circled by the garbage she had pushed away, and was as obvious as if a spotlight had been thrown on it. His eyes focused on her. "You think—"

"You're—"

"Michael Smith," he said, and pursed his lips suddenly. She had the feeling he was biting back a laugh. "Savannah," he drawled, and a tingle of delight danced within her as her hopes raised a fraction. "I owe you another apology. I intended to tell you the truth when I got to know you better, but I think I'd better go ahead and trust you now. Let's sit down." He turned around one of the chairs at the table and held it for her. Then he moved to the one next to it and sat beside her, spreading his knees so hers were between his. He was close, bare-chested, and she forgot about her suspicions and worries.

"I was told by my attorney to keep my identity secret at all costs, so when I first came on board, I told you Miles Seth was my name and that I worked for the Acme Company. I'm Mike Smith and I don't work for Acme, but everything else is true." He leaned forward, resting his elbow on the arm of his captain's chair. He took her hand and placed it on his knee. Spreading her fingers, he ran his thumb over her knuckles, altering her breathing as he talked. His knee was bony beneath her hand, his flesh was warm, and his chest was very close. He wasn't a bank robber. He had told her he was Mike Smith; her fears were gone, and at the moment she was finding it difficult to keep her attention on what he was saying.

"I'm a witness to a crime involving two men. The trial is coming up, and my life has been threatened. While cooperating with the police and the prosecuting attorney, my own attorney has helped me hide and warned me not to tell anyone my identity. He gave me his yacht to use—"

"Oh, mercy! That wasn't your boat!"

"Don't panic. That's why everyone pays insurance premiums. I wish Fitz had his yacht, but I'm glad to be right here." He watched her in silence for a moment, letting her think about what he had said. "Do you believe me?"

"Yes," she said softly. As she looked into his eyes, she realized she would have believed anything he had told her.

"I'm not a bank robber," he drawled, trying hard to hold back his laughter.

She felt her cheeks burn. "You sort of fit the description, and I saw your open billfold when I went in to change the sheets. I saw your name."

"Yeah, well, I should have told you earlier, but I've learned to be highly cautious. What was the description of the bank robber?"

"I'm sorry, but you're over six feet fall, you're male, and Caucasian."

"Scars?" he asked.

When she blushed and nodded, he said, "My scars must have worried you. I got them in the car wreck that killed my wife."

"I'm sorry!"

"Yeah. I'm pretty banged up because of the wreck." He waved his fingers toward his shoulder. "My leg is the worst. Want to see?"

He caught her offguard. "No!" Then she saw the laughter in his eyes and knew he had been teasing. "You didn't mean that! What would you have done if I'd said yes?" she snapped.

"Peeled off my jeans," he said, "and shown you. Any request—"

"Never mind!" she said, laughing. "I walked into that one. Oh, Mike, I'm so glad you're not a bank robber!" She meant it with all her heart. "How long do you have to hide?"

"The trial is a little over two months away."

"Two months! You were going to live on the yacht all that time?"

"Yeah, it seemed to be the best place. The trial is set for the last week in August. I've taken a new job." His features clouded and an angry tone came into his voice, one she hadn't heard since the first few seconds of their fiery encounter outside. "I'm going to have to move elsewhere when the trial is over. The attorneys and police have warned me I won't be safe in Minnesota. I've got a new place to live and a new job lined up—accountant for Jones, Lampkin, and Krebly in Santa Fe, New Mexico. I'm doing work with them now. But at the moment all my work is at the bottom of the lake."

"Oh, no! Your accounting work sank with the boat?"

"Oh, yes. And my pistol, and my glasses—"

"How terrible for you!"

He laughed. "But you're not going to say you're sorry you caused it."

"No, I'm not, because I didn't. Can you see without your glasses?"

He squinted. "Not very well." He trailed his fingers over her face. "You have a nose and hair . . ." His hand slipped rapidly down over her shoulder. "And a throat and—"

"You can see," she said, catching his hand. "You do your work by mail?"

"Yes. It's only a temporary arrangement until the trial. I thought you might have read about me and the trial in the paper."

"I don't recall reading about it."

"Only bank robbers come to mind when you look at me."

"Mike—"

"I'm teasing. I worked for the Monitor National Bank. To simplify what happened, two of the men I worked with, one of them a friend, were falsifying loans and embezzling funds. So far they've discovered four hundred thousand dollars missing. I'm going to testify against them, because I have to if I don't want to lie."

"That's terrible! I mean, of course the crime is terrible, but how dreadful it must be for you to have to testify against a friend."

"Yeah," he said, a frown developing. "The other one has threatened me, and there's been an attempt on my life. That's why I had to be so cautious when I didn't know you, and it's the reason I had to tell you a fictitious name."

"Can't the police help?"

"They're limited. The police don't know who tried to kill me and can't link it to either of the men, who are out on bail. The authorities said I need to stay in hiding until the trial, then make a new start somewhere else."

Every time he talked about starting over again, Savannah heard the bitterness in his voice. She covered his hand with hers, pressing it lightly. "I'm sorry."

He leaned closer, and she became conscious of how inviting his bare chest looked. His fingers curled around hers as he lifted her palm and trailed his lips across it, igniting dancing fires along her veins. He watched her, and she didn't try to hide her quick intake of breath. Drawing nearer to him, she dropped her gaze to his lips.

"I'll be damned glad when your mouth heals," he whispered, and leaned forward to kiss her gently.

"I'm damned glad you're not a bank robber," she whispered, and slipped her arms around his neck as he pulled her onto his lap. He paused to raise his head. His eyelids drooped as he gazed at her, smoldering sensuality visible in his expression. "Savannah, I'll warn you now, I'll never marry again. Never." A shuttered look came over his features. "It hurt too badly to love and lose Leah. I'm not going to get that deeply involved in life again." The look was gone in an instant, and he smiled. "You're not moving away from me."

"I hadn't planned on a proposal tonight," she murmured, momentarily hating the hardness she had glimpsed in his eyes. "I haven't known you twenty-four hours yet."

"And tomorrow and tomorrow?"

She smiled, feeling secure in the knowledge that she led a satisfying life. "We'll part and we'll remember each other. I have a good life, Mike. It isn't empty."

"I'll bet it's not," he whispered, sure there was another man somewhere. "I'll bet it isn't dull, either."

"Oh?"

"You threatened me with an ax, you dug through garbage to see if I was a bank robber . . . The women in my life don't have that much pizzazz."

"I have pizzazz?" she asked, pleased.

"Yeah," he said, looking at her mouth and thinking again that there had to be a man in her life. She was too lovely, too exciting. They had been thrown together by a summer storm, a brief interlude before they had to pick up the threads of their lives and go their separate ways. And as he contemplated going his separate way from Savannah, without conscious thought his arms tightened around her. He pressed her soft body to his bare chest, the vision of her in the wet T-shirt with her full, well-shaped breasts clearly outlined coming to mind and he groaned softly. He kissed her so hard, it made her wimper as he pressed her bruised lip. He stopped at once, kissing her lightly. "Sorry. I got carried away."

"Mike," she whispered longingly, believing every word he had said, relishing touching him, knowing with a woman's instinct that she had found something special in him. She slipped off his lap and stood up. "It's getting late."

He smiled at her, thinking she looked more exciting after she had been kissed. Her cheeks were pink, her lips red, and there was a drowsy, earthy quality to her expression that made him hard with desire, but he curbed the urge to pull her back to him.

As she turned to pick up the soggy paper, he reached down and scooped it up for her.

"You're handy to have around." She smiled, then a strange look crossed her face.

"What is it, Savannah? Is something wrong?"

"No. Where will you stay, now that the yacht has sunk?"

"I'll call my lawyer, and he'll find another place for me." Mike ran his fingers through his curls. "I don't know where I'll go."

"You can stay with me."

His steamy gaze focused on her and the conclusion he had jumped to was blatantly obvious. Hastily, she said, "Not in my room!"

He grinned. "What do you have in mind?"

"You can stay on the houseboat. No one will bother us, because my family and my friends know I want them to leave me to myself for two weeks. I sort of need to recharge my batteries."

His grin changed to a leer. "Oh, darlin', are you inviting me to recharge your batteries?"

"No!" She saw he was teasing and laughed. "Cool your imagination, Mr. Smith!" She sobered just as quickly, speaking in a calm, practical voice, not caring to look too closely at her own motives. "You can stay on the houseboat."

"Thank you," he answered solemnly, feeling his pulse leap at the prospect of staying almost fourteen more days with Savannah. Reluctantly he said, "I might jeopardize your safety."

"That's foolishness! No one can find you if you're staying with me. Really, it's fine."

He explained the risks to her.

"Mike, it's okay," she said.

"I think I'll stay," he said, capitulating without wrangling any further with his conscience. "I need to get in contact with my attorney. I have to be available at all times if the defense lawyers need to depose me."

"Depose you?"

"They have the right to question me—take a deposition—before we go to trial, and I have to be available to them. But I'd like to stay if you'll have me."

She looked into his sky-blue eyes and felt the sexual tension arc between them. Two weeks with a man who had physically and emotionally swept her off her feet! The prospect made her heart quicken, and she smiled at him.

"I'll have you," she said softly, the play on words instantly obvious to them both, making her heartbeat more erratic. She looked into his eyes, wondering what lay ahead for them. If it were anything as explosive as the 'past few hours . . . She felt breathless with anticipation and held out her hand to him, wondering if he thought she was this receptive to every man she met.

A sudden flicker of surprise crossed his face, but was replaced immediately by a satisfied smile as his fingers closed over hers. He leaned close to her. "You trust me?"

"With my life," she answered, and Mike felt as if the earth, lake, and boat had dropped out from under him. He pulled her gently to him and kissed her, trying to remember her injured lip, curbing his impulse to crush her to him and kiss her until she was breathless.

"Shall we go to bed?" he drawled, half-teasing, half-holding his breath to see what she would say. She was as unpredictable as lightning.

"Sure. You to the aft stateroom, and I'll go to the forward stateroom."

"Aw, shucks . . ."

"Don't press your luck," she said in a breathy voice, sending his blood pressure up a notch. "You have a roof over your head, food in the pantry, and someone to talk to during the long hours of the day."

"Believe me, I appreciate . . . the roof, the place, and most of all the someone." His rumbling voice gave a deeper meaning to his words.

" 'Night, Mike."

He kissed her lightly, and whispered, " 'Night, Savannah. Sweet Savannah, who sank my boat and then rescued me."

She smiled and shook her head, then forced herself to turn and walk away instead of flinging her arms around him. He was the sweet one! A man who was as sweet as he could be tough . . . who could make her laugh, who could make her melt with just a word.

She closed the door to her stateroom and listened to the steady beat of rain on the houseboat and the wind that still whistled around the corners.

For hours Mike lay awake in the dark cabin, his hand propped behind his head, while he pondered his reaction to Savannah. It had been instant and intense, making him feel younger, more alive than he had been in a long time. He remembered her holding the ax and he smiled. Then his smile faded as he thought about holding her in his arms while she sat on his lap. Desire escalated, strong enough to make him ache. With a groan he closed his eyes and hoped he would be able to sleep.

When morning's early rays came warm and pink through the portholes, he opened his eyes and stared at the ceiling, seeing the rippling reflection of sunlight play on the wood, momentarily thinking he was on the *Marietta*. A sweet, clear song reached his ears, and he opened his eyes wider—and remembered. While he listened to Savannah singing, he turned on his side and smiled.

Her singing changed to whistling, and then she was silent. He stretched on his back, placing his hands behind his head, his thoughts drifting back over their first moments together. Amusement deepened as he recalled seeing her down on her hands and knees reading through the garbage. A shrill scream pierced the air. Mike bolted up, and his blood turned to ice.

Four

He jumped from the bed, snatching up the first pair of jeans he spotted. He stepped into one leg, and yanked on the other one as he ran toward the sound of Savannah's screams, discovering too late that he had on her brother-in-law's jeans. Clutching them around his middle, he yelled, "Savannah!"

"Mike!"

He heard the panic in her voice. His heart thudded with fright that someone had followed him and was threatening her. He ran outside and along the deck, following the sound of her yells.

"Help! Mike!"

"I'm coming! Where the hell are you?"

"Here!" He reached the end of the deck and looked up. Savannah was on the sun deck, her body outlined against a clear azure sky, her golden hair catching glints of sunlight. She was hugging herself, her eyes round with fright, hopping from foot to foot in agitation. A portion of his brain took note of her faded cut-offs and yellow T-shirt, and of her long, shapely legs. He glanced around and didn't see a sign of any kind of danger, but her face was drained of color and she was scared.

"What's wrong?"

"There's an animal in the kitchen!"

"An animal!"

"In one of the lower cabinets. Some kind of beady-eyed, long-nosed—"

He threw back his head and laughed in relief as the ridiculousness of her actions struck him.

"What are you laughing at?" she snapped. "It looks like a possum or a rat! It hissed at me!"

He laughed harder. "You'll take an ax and try to fight a man you think is about to attack you—a man almost twice your size—and here you are on the roof, screaming and hollering over what's probably a cat or squirrel that came in out of the rain!"

"It isn't funny! Rats are different." She shivered, and he grinned at her.

"You scared the living hell out of me over a cat!"

"You were scared?" she asked, her eyes widening.

"I thought you might have been in danger."

Her frown returned. "I was—I am. I can't cook in the kitchen with a rat!"

"The galley, Savannah. It's called a galley."

"Galley, kitchen—it has a wild animal in it!"

"So what do we do, give him the keys to the boat and abandon ship?"

"It isn't funny!"

He couldn't help teasing her after the fright she had given him, and he couldn't keep from chuckling over the incongruity of her braving his anger and being ready to fight him, yet hightailing it out at the first sign of some little furry varmint, which was probably only a mouse. He got a tighter grip on his loose jeans and grinned at her. "All right, darlin', I'll save you," he drawled, giving a dramatic flourish with one arm. "The dastardly varmint probably came on board last night to get in out of the rain. Never fear, I'll send the dragon back to the island."

"Michael Smith, it isn't funny!"

"I didn't laugh just then."

"It might bite you," she said, sounding truly worried.

"Pshaw! You can hide your eyes and I'll rout the unfortunate critter. How big is it?"

"I think you're still laughing at me!"

"Do you see so much as a smile?" he asked solemnly. "How big is the dragon?"

"Don't call it a dragon! I could cope with a healthy, big dragon that was breathing fire on me."

"I know, you'd get your ax. How big is the beady-eyed monster?"

"Sort of big. I don't know. I saw two beady eyes, a nose, and heard it hiss, and I didn't stay around to get a closer look. I don't like rodents!"

He grinned. "I'll tell you when it's safe to come down."

"Thanks," she said, sounding enormously relieved. He wondered if he would ever understand women even if he lived to be one hundred years old.

He looked around for something to nudge the animal with, easily imagining a mouse scampering to the houseboat on one of the ropes tied to a tree on the island. He picked up a long oar and went inside the galley. The cabinet stood open, and he moved quietly, knowing if it were a mouse it could be burrowed in a tiny hole and he never would find it.

He squatted and stared into the cabinet, but saw two large empty pans and nothing else. Still moving without a sound, he slipped the oar into the cabinet and nudged the pans. Nothing ran out and nothing was behind them. He stood up and looked around the kitchen, sure if he didn't find something, he not only wouldn't eat, he might not get Savannah down off the sun deck. Hunkering down, he peered into the cabinet again. Behind him a scratching noise caught his attention, and he turned. A bit of a black furry tail disappeared around the corner of the open door.

Mike vaulted after it, jumping outside and looking along the deck, sure it was someone's cat and he could reassure Savannah about her safety. There was no sign of an animal. Then he spotted a tub lying on its side, angled against the bulkhead, with a few bits of black fur showing at the rim. Mike flipped away the tub and looked down at beady black eyes, a pointed nose, and black fur with a white stripe—a skunk!

"Skunk!" he yelled, and turned to run at the same moment the skunk bristled. Mike was too late. He had penned the skunk in between the bulkhead, the tub, and himself. He jumped back, and his feet became tangled in a line. As the skunk defended itself in the only way possible, Mike stumbled against a chair, spun around it, and ran a few yards. Holding his nose Mike looked back, to see the skunk waddle to the edge and disappear over the side of the deck. Savannah leaned over the sun deck, watching Mike as he dashed along the deck and ran for the water.

"It's a skunk!" he yelled.

He heard laughter that stopped him in his tracks, and looked up at her. "Dammit, if you laugh at me after sending me to get a skunk . . . You knew what it was!"

"I didn't! I promise, I didn't!"

Staying the length of the deck away from him, she climbed down the ladder and stood fanning the air.

"Whooie, darlin'," she said, drawing out the word and imitating the way he had teased her earlier. "You have to change your after-shave!"

"I think you did that on purpose because I laughed

at you! You knew it was a skunk. I can't stand this! How do I get rid of the smell?"

She shrugged, trying to keep a straight face. "Beats me. I don't know a thing about skunks."

"Oh, damn, this is awful."

"I quite agree." She waved her hands faster and watched as he turned and quickly went over the rail, diving into deep water. He bobbed to the surface, and she sauntered closer to talk to him while he treaded water and swore.

She laughed, waving her hands. "Seems as if I read somewhere, water won't wash off the smell of skunk."

"If you don't stop laughing I will come out of this water and hug you and kiss you and then you'll smell just the same and have the same damned dilemma!"

"Oh, my!"

He frowned at her for a full minute. "Savannah," he said in an even tone that made her suspect his patience had worn thin. "Will you go to my stateroom and get me something, a towel, anything, to wear? Your brother-in-law's jeans fell off when I jumped in, and I can't find them, and I don't think I want to anyway."

"Sure, Mike, anything I can do to come to your rescue, after you routed my black-and-white dragon!" she called merrily, and went inside smiling to herself.

She picked up a towel and a pair of her brother-in-law's torn faded cut-offs. She decided whatever Mike put on when he came out of the water, they might have to burn because of the smell. She hurriedly closed the galley door to shut out the odor from the deck, and returned to the deck. Mike was treading water, waiting patiently. She draped the cut-offs and the towel on the lifeline. "I'll leave you some privacy. Want anything else?"

"Yeah, some perfume."

She laughed, and he grinned back at her. She leaned forward over the lifeline, her hands on her hips, as he swam closer. Wrinkling her nose, she said, "Mmmm, you do smell better! So fresh, so clean."

"You can make amends for sending me after a skunk," he said in a coaxing voice.

"Oh?" her pulse skipped a beat as she looked down into his eyes.

"Come join me?" he asked, the words falling like drops of honey, sweet and enticing.

She shook her head. "Mike, you're getting used to the smell. If you don't mind, thanks for the invitation, but not this time. All the water in the lake can't quite eradicate the faint odor of Mr. Skunk."

"Damn," Mike said mildly, smiling at her.

She walked away, her laughter floating in the air while Mike paddled closer to the houseboat and watched her derriere jiggle provocatively with each step.

It took him another hour to get rid of the smell. Then he drenched himself in after-shave and talcum and finally went to the galley to find her frying bacon and eggs. She sang as she worked, her ponytail swaying lightly as she shook her head in time to the rhythm of her song. He propped one hand on the bulkhead, enjoying listening to her sing, enjoying more the sight of her brief cut-offs, which left little to his active imagination. Her white cotton shirt was tucked into the narrow waistband of the cut-offs—a waist he could span easily with his hands, and wanted to. He smiled, thinking she could be as brave as a tigress and as timid as a rabbit. Music, silent or audible, seemed to surround her.

He had followed the delicious, tempting smells of bacon and hot coffee to the galley, his stomach grumbling and his mouth watering, only to have lost all appetite for bacon and eggs as he watched Savannah. His appetite was far too strong for mere food to satisfy, a deeper hunger.

He silently crossed the room, wanting to surprise her, wanting his arms around her before she turned and placed a barrier of some kind between them.

He rested his hands on her waist, leaned down to kiss the back of her neck, and murmured, "Thank goodness the smell didn't precede me!"

She laughed, dropping the spatula on the counter, and turned to smile at him, her hands on his forearms.

His pulse jumped as he saw that her lip was much better, her dimple showing when she smiled up at him. He wanted to envelop her in his arms and kiss her until the sun went down, and maybe a little longer.

"Thanks for being such a wonderful skunk-slayer," she said, and kissed him on the cheek.

"I don't want to hear another word about that skunk! And the next time you see a pair of beady eyes peering at you—you're going with me to rout the scurvy beast."

She shuddered. "I don't care for rodents."

"Soft little bunnies scare you?"

"No, but beady-eyed rats and long-nosed possums and creepy little mice do."

He smiled down at her, wrapping his arms around her. "Darlin', I'll protect you from four-legged friends that go pitty-pat in the night."

With a shiver of excitement, she slipped her arms around his neck and relished the hug, then tilted her head back to look at him. "This is different from anything I've felt before, Mike."

He sobered at once, looking into green eyes that

echoed her words in their fiery depths. "How's your lip?"

"Better."

"Let's see," he whispered, and leaned down. He still kissed her lightly so he wouldn't hurt her.

The merest touch from him was a beckoning siren, pulling on her senses. Savannah stood on tiptoe and pressed her lips against his. The smell of smoke finally permeated her brain, and she leaned back again.

"I smell smoke."

"Yeah," he drawled. "The skillet's on fire." He kissed her again. Savannah let him until the acrid odor of the smoke became stronger.

"I don't want to burn down the houseboat," she murmured.

"It's too late for breakfast. It's cinders now," he whispered, his hand slipping over her back, lowering to the curve of her spine and creating a breathlessness in her. "One more kiss," he cajoled, "and I'll put out the fire."

"Skunk-router, fire fighter, the best kisser . . ." she whispered.

Minutes later he released her, moving her swiftly away from him, then yanked up a metal lid and slammed it over the flames coming from the skillet. Fanning the smoke and coughing, he stepped back and looked at her. "Fire's extinguished. We'd better air out this place."

"Everything's closed because outside it smells like skunk."

"And in here it smells like smoke," he said, and they both laughed. He crossed the few feet between them to wrap his arms around her. "Who's hungry or wants to breathe anyway?"

"I was thinking about you last night . . ."

"Oh, darlin' . . ." he replied with a suggestive leer.

"I was thinking about your needing a hiding place!" she said firmly. "When I go home, you can come stay with me. I live alone in a house in a nice, quiet neighborhood and I lead a busy life. No one will know you're there, and you should be safe until the trial."

The amused expression left his face, and he looked at her with the smoldering, knee-melting intensity he could develop so swiftly. "You'd do that for me?" he asked hoarsely.

She nodded. "It wouldn't be a chore," she whispered, catching her breath as he leaned closer. His mouth silenced her words. She forgot her injury and stood on tiptoe to wrap her arms around his neck and kiss him for all she was worth.

His arms crushed the breath from her lungs. Finally the kiss became too passionate and she whimpered, bringing an instant cessation to the kiss. He looked down at her, smoothing locks of golden hair away from her cheek.

"I want to say yes, thank you, and never look back, but wherever I go—danger goes." His voice roughened, the look in his eyes becoming as cold as chips of glacial ice. "After I had been threatened, I couldn't believe anyone would actually try anything. I've never had anyone want to kill me before. One night after work I went to a dinner party. I was coming home late, and as I turned the corner into my driveway, a black car started up, moving toward me. It had been parked at the curb, but I hadn't noticed it. Someone shot at me and, fortunately, missed." His voice dropped. "But not by much. I flung myself down on the seat, or I would have been hit, because the person kept on firing. The car smashed against the tree in my yard, but I hadn't been going fast, so the impact was minor. I live in a peaceful neighborhood. Any little thing and the neighbors call the police."

"Oh, Mike, that's terrible!"

His strong jaw hardened and a muscle tensed in his cheek. He had a slightly thin, oval face with prominent cheeks, and there were moments when he looked bitter, angry, and formidable. "What I hate—of course I want to live—but I'm scared for Brian. This summer session of Semester-at-Sea worked out perfectly. When he gets back he's transferring to another university in California, a change he had planned anyway. I'll live in New Mexico instead of Minnesota, and I pray everything will be all right."

"I'm sorry," she said, hugging him, placing her head against his chest and listening to his strong, steady heartbeat. "For an accountant who sits at a desk all day, you have good reflexes," she said, recalling how swiftly he could move.

"I run. I did play baseball on the bank's team, and I went to college on a baseball scholarship."

"You did?" she asked, impressed.

He laughed and flicked his forefinger lightly on the tip of her nose. "Yes, I did. That's not so spectacular."

"I think it is. Where do your parents live? In Duluth?"

"No," he said solemnly, and she noticed how expressive his eyes could be. "My folks died in a boating accident when I was twelve, and I went to live with an uncle. He was an engineer with an oil company, and we moved a lot. Uncle Grant was fourteen years older than my dad, and now he's not well. I wanted him to come live with us, but he wouldn't do it. So he went to a senior-citizen home in St. Paul where he met and married a woman. The police don't think he's in any danger." Mike smiled at her, his hands running lightly back and forth over her shoulders. "Tell me about your family."

"I think I have. There are a lot of us."

"Any pictures here?"

"Sure." She left the galley and returned in seconds with a scrapbook under her arm. He smiled at her and winked, taking the book from her hand, and said, "Before we sit down to look at the family album, let's get something to eat. I'm going to faint soon, if I don't have sustenance."

"Don't you dare faint! That's what caused all the trouble. I was just trying to give you mouth-to-mouth resuscitation when—"

"Oh, darlin', let's try that mouth-to-mouth again," he teased, leaning down.

Laughing, she slanted a look at him. "I thought you were hungry. Breakfast time," she announced firmly. "We're going to eat—interesting conversations or not!"

He grinned and picked up the skillet with the burned eggs to throw out the ashes. "After breakfast I'll look at the motor and try the radio. I have to get in touch with my attorney. Will your family be worried about you?"

She shook her head. "No, not unless something special has happened. They know I'm resting from school and they'll leave me alone. Usually the *Bluebell* is tied to the dock and in no danger from storms."

"And the friends you date?"

She shook her head. "If they can't get me, they won't give it a thought. I don't sit home much."

"I'll bet not," he said, feeling a flicker of relief that there wasn't any one guy of importance.

In minutes they were seated over bowls of cereal, their heads together as they looked at the family album. Savannah pointed out pictures of so many Blair's, Mike's head swam. She showed him pictures of her parents, Maggie and Todd Blair; her three sisters and two brothers and the in-laws; children; and other Blair relatives. As they thumbed through the pictures, he was curious about Savannah's divorce, and when she turned to a page with pictures of her standing beside a handsome, smiling man, Mike was jolted by shock. He turned to stare at her. "You were married to Tyler Carson!"

"Yes. You know him?"

"Yes," he answered, remembering parties where the two had crossed paths. Tyler, a judge, was successful, handsome, likable. Puzzled, Mike studied her a moment, wondering about her marriage and divorce.

"We had career differences," she said quietly. "I see the questions in your eyes." To her surprise, Mike's face flushed.

"Sorry, I didn't mean to pry, and you don't have to tell me anything about it."

"That's all right. Tyler and I couldn't agree, and finally I knew the marriage was over for me. I think it was just as over for Tyler. He didn't understand my views and I couldn't understand his."

"I'm sorry."

"I'm happier now than I have been in a long, long time," she said with unmistakable sincerity.

Mike was still puzzled, wondering how their careers had conflicted. He studied her before he asked, "Is that why you suddenly became a teacher and gave up merchandising and modeling?"

"Yes. Teaching is more satisfying for me. Tyler couldn't understand that."

"He wanted you to pursue your fashion career instead of teaching?"

"Tyler and I divorced; then I went back to school to become a teacher."

Mike still couldn't fit the pieces together, and he

knew the problem must have been something basic and important to Savannah. "Did he know you wanted to be a teacher?" When she shook her head, his curiosity increased. "What was the career conflict, then? You didn't like his career? It took too much time away from you?"

"No." She tugged a bit of frayed string from the edge of her ragged cut-offs. "We married when we were in college and we both had hopes and dreams. When we started to work, Tyler began to make great strides in his career. I achieved a degree of success working at the store—promotions, raises. Finally I wanted a family, and Tyler wanted me to continue devoting all my energies to my job."

"Oh," Mike said flatly, seeing everything at once. Tyler hadn't wanted children, and Savannah had compensated by becoming a teacher. Momentarily he felt a tug on his heart for her. As little as he knew about her, he knew she was warm and giving. He thought of how badly he and Leah had wanted Brian and of what a wonderful son he was, of all the moments of shared joy that diminished any ache or fear or anger over Brian. Savannah had wanted to have children and had missed parenthood because of Tyler. "I'm sorry about your divorce," he said solemnly, feeling compassion over her sorrow at not becoming a mother.

"I've adjusted to the change and I'm happy," she said without remorse, and Mike believed her. She stood up, picking up their cereal bowls. "The day's half gone."

Shocked, he glanced at his watch and saw she was right. He stood up, stretching and flexing his muscles. "First, want to come watch while I work on the motor?"

"You go right ahead. I'm going to scrub the deck again. I once heard ketchup cuts the smell of skunk."

"Anything's worth a try. And save a little for me."

"Sure thing."

"Later I'll try to contact Fitz, my lawyer." As he left the galley he glanced over his shoulder. Her back was to him, and she sang softly as she worked. His gaze drifted slowly down her legs. She paused in her singing, and said, " 'Bye, Mike." He chuckled and left.

They spent the day working on the houseboat. Mike got the motor going, and they slowly chugged back to the spot where the boat was usually moored. As Mike steered toward the dock with Savannah at his side, his gaze swept the area.

It was a private dock, the last in a long line that were yards apart, giving the boat owners privacy and a bit of room. He was relieved that he would be near boats filled with people. "I see how you drifted away—you're the last one, and there was nothing to stop you once the boat had broken loose and the wind had come up."

"I didn't realize what had happened until too late."

"With the motor on the fritz, you couldn't have stopped the *Bluebell* from being caught in the wind. I'll take us in to the dock. You get out and secure her."

"Sure," she said, and she left, moving into the sunshine, which made a golden blaze of her hair. She raised her face to the breeze, her profile to him, and he had to smile. Savannah looked as if she enjoyed every second of the day to the fullest. He knew he didn't have a place in his life for romance. His warning hadn't fazed her, and he suspected she didn't want any deeper an involvement than he did.

The houseboat slowed, gently scraping and bumping the dock as it came alongside. Mike cut the engine and went out to help Savannah secure the lines.

"Savannah! Are you all right?" a man called.

Mike turned to see a man and woman on the next boat. As they waved, a small boy ran down the pier and headed toward the *Bluebell.*

"I'm fine!" she called back, and waved. "They're the Kirks, and here comes Jimmie," she said to Mike.

"Can we tell him I'm Miles Seth?"

"Sure," she said quickly, smiling at him.

Mike hated the deception, but he could remember too clearly the bullet smashing the glass of his car window.

"Hi, S'vannah," a small, freckle-faced boy said, standing on the dock with his hands on his hips.

"Hi, Jimmie. This is Mr. Seth."

" 'Lo. How come you left in the storm? Dad was scared you'd drowned."

"Nope! You tell your dad that the wind blew the *Bluebell* loose, and I've been out on the lake."

"You found Mr. Seth in the lake?"

"Do you want to come in and have an apple and I'll tell you about it?"

"Sure."

"You'd better tell your mom."

"She said I could come down."

Mike was busy with the lines, and looked up when Savannah glanced at him questioningly. "I'll be in when I'm through. You two go ahead."

He watched her walk along the deck, Jimmie's hand in hers, and felt a stab of admiration for the way she had made a new life for herself and filled it with children. He suspected her rapport with Jimmie was repeated countless times in friendships with other children she knew. He began to hum without realizing it, his flat monotone a droning sound. When he finished, he jumped back on board and went to find Savannah and Jimmie.

• • •

Later Mike phoned his attorney. When he came into the stateroom where Savannah was, he looked grim.

"Something wrong?"

He ran his hand over the nape of his neck. "They've discovered more funds missing. It's over eight hundred thousand dollars now. That's a lot of money to have vanished."

"And it means there's more pressure on you, doesn't it?"

He shrugged. "They wanted me dead before. Now they will more than ever. But the results are the same."

"Are you the star witness?"

"Yes. They came to me and wanted to cut me into the deal because of my friend."

"Oh, Mike! Will you have to testify to that?"

"Unfortunately, yes. They knew when—" Abruptly he snapped off his words. "It's water under the bridge now."

She put aside a stack of papers and went to him, placing her hands on his forearms. "No one will find you here."

His gaze shifted to her, and he stared at her blankly for a second, as if he were making an effort to pull his thoughts back to the present. "That's another thing. I told my lawyer about his boat. There'll be insurance papers to fill out. You need to let your brother-in-law know, and find out from him who you should call, but it might focus attention on us. I think you'll be safer if—"

"No," she said, giving a vigorous shake of her head. "You're safe here, and there's absolutely no danger for me. Won't your attorney look out for your privacy and your interests? An insurance man won't announce to the world where you are."

"It's easy to be nonchalant about it when nothing's ever happened to you," he said angrily, and she felt a swift stab of pain for him. She put her arms around him.

"I'm sorry. You hate having to move from Duluth, don't you?"

"Yes," he said in a tone so harsh, it startled her. "There isn't a choice, though. Fitz is handling the sale of my house."

Suddenly he smiled and gently tugged on a lock of her hair. "I don't want to cause you any trouble."

"Don't worry. The Kirks are my closest neighbors here at the dock, they're going home tomorrow and won't be back for two weeks," she said, knowing she was flirting with the real danger of losing her heart to him. Mike was exciting. In the short time she had known him, she realized he had a more intense effect on her than any other man ever had. And he had made clear his intentions—no strings, no commitment, no involvement. She studied his well-chiseled mouth and his thickly lashed eyes, and knew she should be more careful about how deeply she exposed her heart. She had a good, happy, satisfying life. Mike Smith could throw it out of balance so easily. And all the time the arguments were running through her mind, she continued speaking. "It's absolutely safe. We'll have this place to ourselves. Except—"

Her voice became filled with concern. "My family will be here on the last Sunday before I go home. They're all coming out, and two of my brothers and their families are taking the boat when I leave that night."

"Don't you think it would be wiser if I slipped away ahead of time and stayed in hiding?"

She chewed her lip thoughtfully for a few seconds,

then answered emphatically. "No, I don't! I want you to meet my family. They won't harm you."

"I know they won't harm me," he said, leaning closer to her, his arms tightening to pull her to him, "but little by little, more and more people will know I'm here."

"My family can keep its collective mouth shut. I promise," she said, resting her hand lightly on his muscled chest.

He grinned. "Okay." He tilted his head to one side. "Let me show you something." He pulled out his brown leather wallet and flipped it open. From inside he took out a wrinkled and tattered news clipping. He smoothed it and handed it to her. She studied a picture of several men dressed in business suits. She recognized the courthouse in the background. "This is Quenton Young," Mike said, pointing to one person, "one of the men involved." She studied the heavyset man in the photo. He had blond hair, large features, wore glasses, and had a friendly, trustworthy face. Mike pointed to another, a slender, handsome, dark-haired man. "This is Zack O'Toole. We used to be friends. I thought you should have an idea of what they look like."

"I don't remember reading about this or seeing their pictures. I may have been busy with schoolwork."

Mike folded the picture and tucked it away. "Today, after I talked to Fitz, I phoned the company in Santa Fe. They're sending more copies of the work that sank in the lake. I told them to send it to the local post office in care of general delivery. Will you pick up the package for me when it arrives?"

"Sure."

"And stop in a drugstore and get me a pair of glasses. A prescription isn't necessary, about the mildest magnification is all I need. You'll have to run all the errands. You seem to be getting low on groceries, too."

"Oh, you're probably right!" she exclaimed, slipping out of his grasp, and he wished he hadn't mentioned errands and food. "I'll go to the store. My car's here, and there's a store in a little town about eight miles away."

He looked around for paper, and together they made a list. Mike pulled out his wallet and tossed bills on the table.

"I'll get the groceries," she said.

"Not if you give me shelter here," he replied mildly, but she heard the inflexible note of steel in his tone.

"Mike—" She saw his chin raise a fraction and knew he wasn't going to yield. She smiled and folded the money in her hand. "Thanks, stubborn!"

"It's only right," he said with satisfaction, watching as she gathered up her purse and keys. "Savannah . . ." He hesitated, then said, "Look around when you come back. I don't know any way on earth the wrong people could discover I'm here, but just pay attention."

"I will." She smiled at him one last time and left. He went outside to watch her drive away in a red compact car.

As soon as she was out of sight, he studied his surroundings. He looked carefully at the docks, where boats shone in the sunlight, at the cars parked on a stretch of paving where the road ended in a cul-de-sac, and at the pine-covered land sloping down to the lake. It looked as peaceful and harmless as a painting, yet he knew how swiftly it could change. Deciding everything was all right, he shifted his attention to the *Bluebell* and returned to the stateroom.

As he stepped inside, his gaze fell on the ax, propped against the bulkhead. He smiled and carried it outside to where it belonged. He looked at it a moment, remembering when Savannah had been ready to swing at him. He held it over his shoulder, laughing as he set it back on its hooks. Looking around, he squared his shoulders and headed for the galley to work.

The clutter was amazing. He thought of his own simple house. Leah had been scrupulously neat, and he was the same. While it was scrubbed and clean, the *Bluebell* was a floating storehouse of junk. As Mike straightened the galley, he pushed aside boxes of rocks, shells, and dried flowers that looked as if they had been collected in another century. When he finished the galley, he decided to clean and oil the motor. It was caked with grease, due to neglect, and he suspected untidiness ran in Savannah's family.

As the sun's rays slanted across the deck, he finished and went above to wait for her. In another half hour the red car appeared, and he hurried to meet Savannah and carry the groceries.

Five

As she entered the galley, Savannah stopped so swiftly, Mike almost collided with her.

"What happened?" she asked.

He moved around her and put down the bags of groceries. "I tidied up."

Her melodic laugh sounded above the rustle of paper sacks. "You're fighting a losing battle, Mike!"

"I had to keep busy."

"You might find more satisfaction in fishing. There's plenty of gear."

"I know. I'll get to that later." He took her shoulders and turned her toward a cabinet. "Over there are the rock collections, and the shells, and the dead weeds. Remembering how Brian used to protect his collections, I figured your nieces and nephews might want to save them."

Her eyes sparkled. "I'm sure they would, but the shells and the rocks are mine."

"You saved them from when you were a little girl?"

"From last year, probably. I'm a collector." She brushed past him, celery and green peppers in her hands. "Rocks, shells, books—"

"Hearts," he said, thrusting out his arm to block her path.

Her green eyes widened as she looked up and shook her head. "No, not hearts. Tyler wasn't hurt."

"I missed you," Mike said, and her pulse skipped a beat. It was a statement that sounded as personal as a remark about the weather, but it was so simple and filled with truth that her breath caught.

He took the peppers and celery from her while she remained pinned in place by the look on his face. He focused on her mouth, and she wanted his kiss badly. He moved closer, watching her steadily.

Shivers of anticipation ran through her as his head dipped and his lips brushed hers. A deep wave of passion and longing rocked through her to her toes. She curled her arms around his neck, opening her lips for his thrusting tongue. His kisses set off tremors of response within her as she strained against him, relishing the feel of his long body, the strength of the arms wrapped around her. His hands followed the curve of her back to her waist, drifting lower to pull her hips closer as he bent over her. She felt his hard maleness and within minutes knew they must stop.

"Mike," she said shakily, pushing lightly against him.

Slowly he released her, his eyes smoldering with fire as he watched her with a look that seemed to go to her soul.

It took all her will to step out of his arms. Her breathing was erratic, and she didn't trust herself to speak, fearing he would see how deeply affected she was by his kiss.

She turned to pick up the celery and peppers, and put them away without a word, her thoughts churning over the swift blossoming of the attraction between them. He wouldn't marry. He'd already warned her, a polite way of saying he wanted only casual relationships, she reminded herself as she swiftly put away the groceries. She cast a glance at Mike, debating with herself about him. Then she shrugged. She had already invited him to stay. So be it. She would survive, because she always had.

The corner of his mouth raised in a crooked smile, and he came across the galley to stand near her.

"What's running through your mind?" he asked.

"Not anything that matters."

"Liar," he chided gently. "You're thinking about our making love."

Her mouth opened in surprise as her cheeks became hot. He leaned down to look directly into her eyes. "I was right."

"Don't look so smug!" she snapped, turning away from him and gathering an armload of groceries.

His deep chuckle teased her senses. "I don't think *smug* is the right word. *Happy* is better," he said softly.

She turned to smile at him. "I am, too, Mike."

He started across the narrow space between them, but she sidestepped. "Don't go too fast. We barely know each other."

He seemed to be trying to exercise some control, looking as if he were having an inner struggle with himself. For just an instant a dark, angry look had crossed his features, and she realized there wasn't much time for them. He would stay with her until the trial, then go out of her life forever. And the thought caused surprising pain. She tilted her head to look at him, knowing Mike had become someone very special in her life.

"You keep me at arm's length," he said, "then you look at me like that."

"Like what?" she asked, startled, unaware that she had been staring at him.

There was a long pause, and then he asked, "Want to swim?"

"The water's cold!" she exclaimed, thankful he had dropped the personal conversation.

"Sissy."

"That does it! I can swim if you can."

"Oh, brother. You can't stand a challenge, huh?" he said teasingly.

"Not without trying to meet it!" she said, her eyes sparkling

He set down the canned goods he held in his hands. Hastily she started out. "See you in the water! Last one in is a rotten tomato!"

She heard his chuckle floating after her. In her stateroom she pulled on a black one-piece bathing suit that plunged in the back, with the front cut in a V neckline that revealed the soft curve of her breasts. She plaited her hair, snatched up a towel, and hurried outside to find him already in the water.

"Hi, tomato," he called. "But definitely not rotten!"

"How cold is it?"

"Not too cold for me."

She flung down the towel, sat on the edge of the boat, dipped her toes in the water. "Ahh!"

He grinned. "Too cold?"

"Of course not."

"I don't see you jumping in."

"I have to ease into it."

"Scaredy-cat."

She wrinkled her nose at him and scooted closer, letting water come up to her knees as he swam near.

"Jump in. Chicken!"

She gave him a mock glare and pushed away from the boat, springing into the water where Mike was paddling. She heard his yelp before she hit the cold water. Then she surfaced to see him grinning at her.

"Want to race?" he asked.

"Sure. Name the distance."

"To the buoy and back. You can say go. The loser cooks dinner."

She nodded, yelled go, and swam for all she was worth. Mike passed her easily, reaching the buoy yards ahead of her and waiting until she got there.

"Don't do me any favors!" she snapped.

"My, you're touchy. Okay . . ." He passed her again and swam yards ahead until he was halfway back to the boat. Then she began to catch up, passed him, and touched the boat and won. He swam up as she glared at him.

"You let me win deliberately."

"Of course not. I wore out."

"Now you're lying!"

"And I'm cooking dinner tonight."

"You cheat!"

"I can't take you out, but I can cook."

"You cheated, so it doesn't count."

"You're not really angry, are you?" he asked, suddenly sounding worried and solemn.

"Furious! I don't like cheats who do sneaky things."

Mike studied her, wondering if she meant what she said. "Okay. Let's make up," he said swiftly, swimming close enough to put his arms around her.

"Hey!" she exclaimed, then looked into his eyes. His broad shoulders were covered with silver beads of water. His powerful chest was wet, the mat of dark hair clinging to it damply. Drops of water were sparkling like crystals on his long lashes, and his gaze was on her mouth. He was so desirable, she thought. He looked at her in a way that insulated her from the cold water "Cheat," she whispered, wanting him to kiss her, raising her mouth to his.

If their kisses had been explosive when they were on the boat, they were cataclysmic in the water. He held her, paddling with his feet, moving them to where their toes touched bottom, so they could stand. Her body molded to his, and she felt his hard muscles as his hands moved over her hungrily. His fingers hooked beneath the straps of the swimsuit, and he tugged it down to her waist. Only her shoulders were out of the murky water, and her breasts were milky shadows beneath the brown surface and Mike looked down at her. Her throbbing peaks were against his warm chest as his big hands cupped her fullness and raised her just enough to bring each eager bud out of the water. His thumbs flicked over them, and she gasped. She closed her eyes as her hands drifted over him, down to his hips, and down to his thighs. She heard his swift intake of breath.

"This is too fast, Mike," she whispered.

"I'll give you time. I promise. And I won't cheat. Trust me."

She opened her eyes to look at him, hearing a tender note in his voice that made her quiver like a young willow in the wind. "I do trust you," she said, and realized again that Mike was special. Very, very special.

He leaned down, his tongue touching her lips with the scalding heat of a flame. She closed her eyes, winding her arms around his neck and taking him at his word. Trust.

He kept his word. With a groan he finally pulled her straps in place and swam away from her at top speed. She couldn't catch up with him until he stopped to wait for her.

When they climbed out she glanced at him, and at the sight of his powerful body, his tanned skin, and scant cut-offs she felt tension coil inside her. He looked at her, his eyes narrowed, and said, "Sorry I'm so scarred up. Hope I didn't scare you."

She had noticed the scars—it would have been impossible not to—but the white ridges lacing his left leg didn't detract from his appearance or from his strong muscles and well-shaped calf. She met his eyes and walked over to him, letting her hands drift over the scar on his jaw, down over the one on his shoulder, and down over his hip. Her tone was a throaty whisper as she said, "That wasn't why I was staring."

His eyes darkened, and suddenly he crushed her hard against his chest. He kissed her deeply, bending her backward, then swung her up to release her. "I'm glad I don't repel you," he said hoarsely.

She smiled then, her dimple appearing along with a twinkle in her eyes, and Mike knew he had to put some distance between them or he would lose all control. She was adorable, enticing, and all woman. And he believed her when she said his scars didn't repel her.

"If you're going to trust me and I'm going to keep my promise, you'd better go—quickly!"

"Yes, sir!" she said, laughter in her voice, and left with a provocative wiggle to her hips that he suspected might have been a little more obvious than usual.

Humming off-key as he worked, he made a tossed green salad, steamed broccoli, cornbread, and wild rice to go with the fish Savannah had bought.

When the fish was about done, he called to her, "Dinner in just a few min—"

She appeared in a pale yellow dress that clung to her curves, the soft material swirling around her legs as she walked. She wore yellow pumps and a single gold chain around her neck. Along with a scooped neckline, the bodice of the dress had tiny

white buttons to the waist. Her golden hair shim-
mered, swaying slightly with each step. Mike's mouth
became dry and words died in his throat, as he
forgot where he was or what he had been about to
say.

"Can I help?" she asked.

He pulled his wits together and smiled, shaking
his head as he motioned toward a chair. "Want a
glass of wine?"

"Thank you," she said, sitting down and crossing
her legs. She looked up expectantly, and he remembered he was supposed to be cooking dinner. He
turned to finish, and shortly he led her outside,
where he had set the table. A cool breeze came across
the lake, the air crystal and crisp. A crane flapped
and slowly rose from the edge of the water, disappearing above the dark tops of the pines. Mike
watched the bird, briefly feeling a deep satisfaction
he hadn't known in a long time.

While they ate they talked about her remedial-
reading classes, but all the time Mike wanted to
fling aside dinner and pull her into his arms.

Aching to hold her, he settled for just looking at
her, and enjoyed talking to her until she asked,
"When you move to Santa Fe will you know anyone?"

"Only my employers," he said, feeling the tight
knot of anger that came every time he thought about
pulling up roots and moving, leaving behind all memories and friends. "I met them when I was in Santa
Fe a little while ago."

She stared into space a moment. "I can't imagine
moving. My whole family has lived here since the
first of our relatives came from Sweden in the 1800s."

"Well, I know what it's like to move," he said bitterly, and she focused on him.

"You said your uncle moved around a lot."

"We never did settle in any one place for very

long. When Leah and I married, we thought we were putting down roots in Duluth forever. Shows you can't plan ahead. I planted trees at home that I've watched grow. There are so many memories my home holds for me. . . . I hate to give them up," he said roughly. "It seems so damned needless—all because I'm a law-abiding citizen and won't commit perjury in a courtroom. Because of that I have to tear up roots, say good-bye to old friends . . ." He rubbed his hand across the back of his neck. "I didn't mean to make a speech."

"That's all right," she said quickly, wondering whether he'd revealed his feelings to anyone before.

As if his thoughts were the same as hers, he said, "It helps a little to tell someone about it."

"Does your son mind moving?"

"No. Brian's young and takes things in stride, and he's ready to leave home anyway. He's growing up, and he'll go wherever a job takes him, which is the way I want it. I'd hate for him to be tied to home, but for me it's different."

"None of my family has ever moved away. Talk about roots! Ours go so far down I don't think any of us could pull them up."

"That's nice," he said wistfully.

"You can put roots down again."

"Yeah, and I intend to. After I get to know people and the place, I want to go into business for myself. I want to be my own boss from now on. That's one thing I learned from this."

Without thinking about what she was doing, she placed her hand over his. The touch stirred her more than she would have guessed. His eyes darkened as he turned his hand over to catch hers and raise it to his mouth for a kiss.

"Mike, dinner—" she said breathlessly as his breath fanned over her palm.

If he heard her, he gave no heed. He stood up and pulled her into his arms. "I can't keep my hands off of you. I want to talk to you, to kiss you, to—"

She groaned and stood on tiptoe, brushing her lips against his. His arms tightened around her instantly and his head came down in a surging kiss that lengthened until she had lost all rational thought.

He kept his word and stopped, turning away and going inside abruptly. She let him go, knowing that if they stayed near each other they wouldn't be able to resist taking up where they left off. She stared at the empty doorway and knew to her soul that Mike Smith was a very special man. And her choices were gone; she suspected he already had her heart. It was only a matter of time until he possessed her body.

The thought rocked her, and she sat down, staring thoughtfully into space. She wasn't protected at the moment, and she realized she ought to see her gynecologist, Dr. Borden, soon and go back on the Pill.

She picked up her dishes and carried them inside, and as she cleaned the galley, her thoughts were on her feelings for Mike, on his attitude about commitment.

Days ran together. It was an interlude in her life that held magic in each moment. They fished, they swam. Mike got his mail and a pair of glasses, and he spent several hours each day working on accounting. They kissed and Mike kept his word, stopping when she pushed him away, groaning with reluctance and desire as the flaming need between them escalated steadily.

Their last Sunday on the boat came, the twenty-second of June, and he dressed in the shirt and jeans he had worn when he had climbed aboard the

Bluebell. He met her family, learning their names swiftly as he shook hands with Ray and Pete, her brothers; Ginny, Paris, and Brit, her sisters; the sisters-in-law, Adrienne and Sally; Ginny's husband, Ted Udell; as well as the other brothers-in-law, Van and Logan. Hopelessly lost when it came to remembering names, he met Savannah's parents, Maggie and Todd Blair, and over a dozen nieces and nephews.

They swam, grilled fish, and in the afternoon they all played softball on the bank. Savannah watched Mike pitch to her twelve-year-old nephew. He gave the boy an easy, curving ball that Frank hit. Mike reached out to catch the ball, and as muscles flexed in his long arm, she knew he'd deliberately let the ball slip off his fingertips and go past him to give Frank a chance to make it to first base.

Mike, as well as her brothers, was stripped to the waist. Her brothers wore swim trunks and Mike wore his jeans, and it was difficult for her to keep her gaze from roaming across his broad chest and down over the jeans that molded his well-muscled legs. It was impossible to keep from remembering what it felt like to be pressed against his legs, feel his hard thighs on hers. As Frank made it to first base, Mike turned and looked at Savannah sitting on the sidelines. She winked at him and he smiled, then turned his attention to Pete, who was up next.

This time it was no easy pitch, and Pete missed twice, finally hitting the ball before the third strike. Mike jumped and caught it, putting Pete out. Savannah was up at bat next.

She was only a fair player, but if Mike pitched to her the way he did to the kids, she hoped she would land the ball so deep in the woods he'd never find it. She gripped the bat, waited, then realized he was waiting longer than usual. She took her eyes off the ball to look at him, and he pitched to her.

She swung too late, and had her first strike.

Amused, fuming, she gripped the bat tightly and vowed she wouldn't fall for another one of his tricks. At least he was pitching the same way he had to Pete! Again there was too long a pause. She wasn't going to take her eyes off the ball. Nosirree! Gorgeous blue eyes or not, she would be ready for the pitch! Michael J. Smith was a rascal through and through. She couldn't help herself. The pull was like a pin beside a giant magnet. She had to look at him.

"Strike two!" Ted called, and she glared at her brother-in-law.

"Keep your eye on the ball, Savannah!" Pete yelled.

Mike was grinning at her. She gave him as fierce a glare as she had given Ted. "Cheat!" she muttered under her breath.

Frank watched Mike, then suddenly ran for second base. Mike turned, pitching the ball. The second baseman was Savannah's niece, ten-year-old Alexa, who missed the ball. Frank made it to third before Alexa got the ball back to Mike.

He turned to face Savannah, a mocking grin on his face.

She wrinkled her nose and wished they were alone. She wanted to tell him what she thought about his pitching tactics and she wanted to be kissed. One more strike and she would be out. She intended to keep her eye on the ball this time!

Again Mike waited, and she gritted her teeth, watching the ball every second until finally he threw. Determined to get even with Mike, she swung with all her might. The bat connected and the ball sailed high, past Alexa and into the field.

Frank made it to home base, and Savannah reached second while her team cheered. She gave Mike a triumphant smile. He winked and turned to pitch to

Ted junior, who was put out at first base, and the teams changed sides. As Savannah walked toward the bench, Mike caught up with her.

"You dirty cheat!" she said softly.

He grinned at her, dropping his arm possessively over her shoulders. "Whatever could you be talking about? I played fair and square."

"The heck you did!" she said, her anger only a tease as they reached the sidelines. She turned to face him, conscious that his arm still rested on her shoulder. "You know you made me take my eyes off the ball!"

"I didn't!"

"You did so, and don't act so innocent!"

"How did I do that?" he asked with even greater innocence.

"You made me look at *you*!"

"And that made you miss a pitch! Some people will use any excuse," he drawled, his eyes wrinkling. "All I did was pitch a ball."

"Hah!"

"I think some of your family is staring at us."

"That might be," she said without taking her eyes from Mike.

"You have a nice, nice family."

"They like you."

"Thank you. I can't imagine anyone your family doesn't like," he said dryly.

"They no longer like Tyler," she said, then wished she hadn't brought Tyler into the conversation. Mike didn't seem to notice as his gaze held hers with the same tenacity he had practiced on the pitcher's mound.

"Come with me to get my camera."

"Sure," she said, barely noticing what he had asked.

He slipped his arm across her shoulders again while he called to Pete, "We'll be right back."

They walked to the boat, her step matching Mike's long stride. She was on deck before it dawned on her that Mike didn't have a camera. She stopped in her tracks to stare at him.

"You're at it again! You really are a sneak. You don't have a camera."

"What do you know! So I don't. My camera is at the bottom of the lake, where you sank it!"

"I did not sink your boat!"

"Since we're here—come with me a minute and I'll show you what I intended all along."

Her pulse skipped as she stepped inside the quiet, cool boat, out of the sunlight and away from the crowd of relatives. Mike's arms went around her instantly.

"You're the most gorgeous batter that ever stepped up to the plate," he murmured. "If you had known what was in my thoughts when you faced me . . ."

"Cheating was in your thoughts," she murmured, her gaze on his full underlip. Then her eyes closed and she clung to him while his velvet-soft lips were on hers, pressing and shifting to scrape her mouth deliciously. His tongue thrust into her mouth, touching the inside of her lower lip, taking and giving at the same time until she thought she would melt in his arms.

"Mike," she finally said, pushing at him. "We'd better get back."

He nodded. "You go ahead. I'll be out in a minute. I don't think you want me walking out with you right now."

Without glancing down at his jeans, she knew he was hard with desire. She turned and left, realizing each time it was more difficult to stop. As she rejoined her family, she thought about Mike and how well he had fit into the group. Better than Tyler ever had. Tyler had never been at ease around the children, something she should have noticed early in their relationship, but hadn't. Mike was like one of the family, and he seemed to enjoy them as much as they did him. She had overheard him talking to Pete about the impending trial and knew he had confided in her brother about his identity. At the last minute they had decided to forget about introducing him as Miles Seth, so all the family knew he was Mike Smith.

She had told Pete everything, asking him to see to it that no one talked about Mike when they went back to Duluth.

Finally they ate grilled hamburgers, and after dinner she looked around to find Mike seated in a folding chair, four-year-old Kevin on his lap, while he showed the child how to tie his shoelaces. Mike's dark head was bent close to Kevin's, and Kevin listened, trying to follow instructions. With Mike's encouragement and coaching, the lace finally was tied, and Mike patted a beaming Kevin on the shoulder.

With a pang that hurt, she thought what a wonderful father he must be to Brian, and if only . . . *If only . . .*

The thought of Mike as the father of her child made her head spin. Mike said he wouldn't marry again because it hurt too much, but he had the problems of the world on his shoulders right now, problems that added to his hurt over the loss of his wife. Any man who was so family-oriented, who wanted roots, who obviously loved children, couldn't shut himself away from life.

She watched him thoughtfully, knowing in her heart that Mike was too alive, too much of a man, to withdraw forever from a full life. Did he feel as deeply for her as she did for him? she wondered, knowing that she was irrevocably in love with him. A glimmer of an idea rocked her.

He looked up, meeting her curious stare. His brows arched, and his gaze held hers until she blushed beneath his scrutiny. Her parents interrupted them, to tell everyone good-bye. All the Blairs left who were going back to Duluth. Finally, Mike and Savannah piled into her car and started home.

Her house was hot and stuffy when she opened the door on the darkened interior. She switched on lights, and Mike followed her inside, looking all around him as he walked. The same clutter that had filled the houseboat filled her house, and he smiled, thinking Savannah knew how to enjoy life. She hummed as she walked around the living room turning on lights. His amused gaze went over tables piled with magazines and bookshelves stuffed to overflowing with shells, books, and miscellaneous items. A sewing basket rested on the blue chintz sofa, a partially made quilt thrown negligently beside it. Papers filled a rocking chair, and records and tapes were strewn across a cabinet that held a stereo and television.

"This is home," she said. "Come on. I'll show you your room."

To his delight, she had a king-sized water bed. He sat down on it and patted it. "I'm surprised you have a water bed."

"My nieces and nephews love it, so I put it here in the spare room. They stay with me on weekends. I inherited it from Ginny when they got new bedroom furniture." She opened a chest of drawers and pulled out fresh navy sheets to put on the bed.

"Come over here," he said in a husky voice.

Her heart jumped, and she paused only a second, then crossed the room, letting him pull her down beside him. In seconds he swung her onto the bed, her long golden hair spilling out behind her. He rolled on top of her as he kissed her.

Desire exploded inside her like dry kindling beneath a flame, and she clung to him, her hips writhing and straining against his hardness. She relished the weight of his big, strong body, the length of him stretched out over her. His maleness pressed against her, a hot demand that she wanted to yield to with all her heart.

Suddenly he pushed off her and stood up. His broad chest heaved as he breathed raggedly. "It's getting damned difficult to keep my promise to you," he said, his voice raspy.

She wanted Mike as she had never wanted anyone. She looked at him lovingly, her body trembling with desire. His chest expanded, and his jeans were swollen with his obvious need for her. "I'm a grown woman and I'm able to take care of myself," she said softly. "I won't hold you to the promise any longer."

His eyes narrowed, and she had the feeling he might have taken her statement as an invitation. She wanted to be absolutely sure, so she stood up reluctantly. "Want to see my room?" she asked.

After a long, tension-filled moment he nodded, and she led him to the next room. He paced around looking at her bed, the clutter of half-finished projects, and a collection of paperweights and music boxes. He turned to smile at her as he picked up a music box and wound it, setting it down while it played "Auld Lang Syne."

He came across the room and put his hands on her arms. "Is there anything you don't like or collect?"

"Sure, too much to name."

"I don't believe you."

"You're playing a New Year's Eve song for old acquaintances."

"That's what we'll be on New Year's Eve this year." He leaned closer. "And I hope you're standing in my arms while we both listen to it being played."

His lips brushed hers, and his kiss was sweeter than wine, more steamy than the most tropical jungle. Shaken by what he had just implied, she kissed him with fiery abandon, realizing she responded more strongly to Mike than she could remember ever responding to Tyler. And she loved him more deeply. It was instinct, a feminine knowledge as old as time. This was *the* man for her. She felt as if she had been put on earth to love Mike and be loved by him.

She had relieved him of responsibility for his promise, so this time she firmly stopped him and moved away, wanting to wait and not rush their physical relationship, because it would be the final and complete giving of her heart to him, no matter what lay ahead.

Nights had been disturbing on the boat, but they were more so in the quiet house, with Mike's bed on the other side of the wall from hers. On Friday, the end of the first week, he came into the kitchen with a solemn look on his face.

"Savannah, I've talked to Fitz and I have to go into town. I have to see the lawyers again."

"I'm sorry," she said, hating the harsh look on his face.

"What's worrying me is that I might lead someone back here. I think—"

She stopped him, swiftly pressing her hand over his lips. "No! You come back here, where you're safe!"

"I have to go on Monday, but I can't go in this pair of jeans."

"You're not going home?"

"No. I'd rather buy new clothes, but even that's risky."

"Can I get them for you?"

"Yes. I'll give you my sizes. I've already made a list of what I want."

After breakfast she took the list and kissed him good-bye, leaving with cash he had received in the mail from his lawyer.

She bought a suit, two white shirts, two ties, shoes, socks, shorts, jeans, T-shirts, and a robe. She kept her appointment with Dr. Borden, talking at length with him before she left with a prescription.

Six

On the last Monday in June Mike left in her car. She knew he planned to drive to a grocery-store parking lot, leave her car, and meet Fitz to ride with him.

She found it difficult to concentrate on anything, alternately staring at the clock and wondering what Mike was doing and worrying about him. By now she knew his favorite dish was spaghetti, and she had planned to make it for dinner. Without thinking about motives, she cleaned the living room, bringing a degree of neatness to the room that was unusual. At four she bathed and dressed, putting on a straight red cotton sundress with narrow straps. Finally she heard a car turn into the drive, and she rushed to open the back door.

Mike climbed out of the car, and she drew in a sharp breath, remembering that her first impression of him had been of a gangster. He looked angry and sinister enough now to convince anyone to get out of his way. His jaw was set, his lips were drawn into a hard line, and there was a ruthless determination in his long stride. He looked powerful, invincible, and furious.

Then for the first time he looked up and saw her. His step slowed and his stormy gaze lowered, traveling over her body like rough fingers undressing her swiftly. He strode up the walk and into the kitchen, and she wrapped her arms around him.

"Are you all right?"

"Yes," he said in a clipped voice. She knew he was angry and she suspected he didn't want to talk at the moment. She stood on tiptoe and brushed her lips over his.

"We'd better lock the damned door," he said roughly. He closed it and looked for long moments at the drive.

She hurt for him. Whatever the day had brought, it must have been bad. She ran her hand across the nape of his neck, his curls brushing her fingers like strands of silk.

He turned to look down at her, and she gazed into eyes burning with need. As she reached for him, he crushed her to his lean hardness, and he kissed her as if it were the first kiss he had been allowed in years.

It was no lazy, teasing kiss, no controlled touch, but a bruising, hungry longing that was blatant in its demands.

It took her breath away and her heart pounded, roaring in her ears. His tongue thrust deeply into her mouth, setting her aflame, making her want to yield and give until all his anger and need were gone. She burned from the passion in his kisses. Her hands slipped beneath his coat and across his muscled chest, seeking the warmth of his flesh. She twisted a button free, then another.

He tore his mouth away, the scalding look he gave her as disturbing as his kisses. Without a word he swung her into his arms and carried her to her room.

The room was dusky, with the blinds drawn and the late-afternoon sun slanting in through the windows, but Savannah didn't notice. Mike placed her on the bed, then watched her while he peeled off his coat and yanked away his tie, tossing them down.

He felt starved for her. His gaze swept over her golden hair, which was a tangle behind her head. Her slender arms were bare and tanned, the soft rise of her breasts tempting. He slipped off her shoes, dropping them on the floor. Her lips were parted, her breathing uneven. Her languid, sensuous gaze made his blood heat. He knew she had wanted to wait, and in the past few days he had understood her sentiments and been able to exercise restraint. But now he was wracked with a need for her—all of her. Through the agonies of the day, he had faced new questions from the lawyers that obviously indicated Zack was trying to muddy Mike's reputation, and during that time, again and again, erotic images of Savannah had flitted through his mind.

His need had been growing for days, and control had become increasingly difficult. When she had opened the door to greet him, obviously dressed and perfumed to please him—he wanted to take her right there inside the doorway of the kitchen!

Needing her with an insatiable desperation that he hadn't known before, he sat down beside her and pulled her to a sitting position. With shaking fingers he unfastened the zipper down the back of her dress and yanked it to her waist. His heart slammed against his ribs. She hadn't worn a bra, and her full, lovely breasts were bare, their peaks hard, even though he hadn't even touched her.

His blood was pounding in his ears, and he couldn't wait. He leaned down to take a soft nipple in his mouth, teasing with his teeth, trying to remember to be gentle, but finding it impossible.

Her hands tore at his clothing. Her haste and urgency were as compelling as his, and soon they both were bare, clinging to each other, moving apart to explore and discover, and Mike knew he couldn't wait or savor the moment.

The violence of his lovemaking stirred Savannah to a frenzy. She wanted him as badly, as wildly as he seemed to want her. His body was virile, tanned, his chest furred, his legs covered with short, dark hair, and they felt rough, tingling against the smoothness of hers. His scars seemed to fit with the toughness he sometimes revealed, and they didn't detract from his sensuous appeal.

"I've wanted you since the first night," he murmured against her flesh. "You're mine tonight, Savannah."

His words burned, creating their own sorcery in her bloodstream. His hands touched her intimately, and she cried out in ecstasy. Then he was over her, parting her legs.

"Savannah, I can't wait . . . Next time . . ."

She gasped while she stroked his hips, her hand moving to his throbbing maleness, touching him, making him shake. He drew a sharp breath and lowered his weight, and Savannah welcomed him.

"I can't slow down," he whispered, showering her throat with kisses as her hot, tight warmth enveloped his sex. Dimly he realized she hadn't been with a man in a long time. "Put your legs around me," he commanded as he moved in a rhythm that was as urgent as his foreplay had been.

The roaring in her ears became as fierce as hurricane winds, obliterating everything except Mike and sensation after sensation that rocked her. She cried his name, clinging to him, her hands raking his back as he nipped her shoulder and whispered her name over and over.

"Savannah!" Suddenly he groaned and shuddered with his hot release. Her hips strained against him, rising, thrusting to hold him while she clung to him with love bursting in her heart.

Their bodies rocked together and finally quieted. He held her tightly, his weight a welcome heaviness. He rolled on his side, taking her with him, holding her pinned against him while he kissed her cheek and throat and murmured endearments.

"I waited as long as I could wait. How damned difficult that damned promise was to keep! And how glad I was when you let me out of it."

She stroked his damp back, adoring the smooth skin, the powerful muscles beneath. "Mike, I love you," she whispered, giving freely and totally.

"Ah, Savannah," he murmured against her flesh. "You're sunshine and fire, and I need you. Lord, I need you!" He raised himself up on one elbow to look at her, and she gazed up with wide green eyes.

Mike wanted to look at her forever. She was the most beautiful woman he had ever known. She was sunny and trusting, and if he hadn't told her from the first moment his feelings about a permanent commitment, he would have hated himself right now. But she knew and she loved anyway. He adored her for her giving, caring nature, for her passion, which was so wild, it took his breath away to think about it. He trailed his finger over her incredibly soft skin down between the curves of her breasts. As he looked at her, thinking he could go on forever looking at her, he realized he was beginning to care deeply for her. More than he had dreamed possible. "Love, love . . ." he whispered, and leaned forward to plant an affectionate kiss on her midriff while he savored the new realization.

With a mild sense of shock he remembered that she hadn't been with a man in a long time. He had assumed that because of her loving nature there had been others, but the realization that he was special stirred feelings deep inside him and made him want to crush her to him and shower her with kisses.

"You make me feel twenty again," he whispered, cupping her full breast, his thumb flicking across the peak while he watched for her reaction.

Her hips moved, shifting and pressing against him tightly. He thought he knew his own body, but Savannah evoked a response in him that was beyond anything he had ever known with a woman. Amazed at how swiftly and strongly his desire was rekindling, he leaned down to take a rosy bud in his mouth, to suckle and tease while his fingers found that erotic place that made her gasp and thrust her hips against him. And then it started to build in him again, a need as wild and consuming as before, as violent in climax, until they cried out in unison.

This time, they sank down on the bed and Mike rolled beside her, pulling her against him, cradling her head on his shoulder. "I'm so young with you," he said softly, stroking damp strands of golden hair away from her face. "The years roll back and are gone. The worries of the present become nothing."

"I'm glad," she said, gazing at the man she loved with all her heart. She sat up suddenly, wanting to look and look and never stop. Secretly she prayed that out of their joining she would have part of Mike forever, the baby she had always wanted, Mike's child.

"Mike, what happened today that was so bad?"

"I received a call while I was with the lawyers. They swear they don't know how anyone found me. Someone, just an anonymous, raspy voice, threatened Brian."

"Oh, Mike." She held him tightly while he talked with his lips against her, his words muffled. "Fitz told me not to worry; we called Brian from his office. He had a copy of Brian's itinerary, and for once we were able to reach him at a hotel. He's fine, he's having fun, but it just tore me apart."

"Try and forget, because Brian is safely out of the country and all right."

"It makes me so damned angry. I'd like to get my hands on whoever is doing this to me!"

"You know my family would gladly go to the trial to give you moral support."

"Thanks, but it will be safer for everyone if they don't. I don't want anyone to realize I know you. I want you safely out of everything involved in the case."

"Okay, but they can be good support."

"I can imagine. You're lucky, Savannah, to have such a close-knit family." He brushed his hand over her hair, thinking how satisfied she was with her career and her large, loving family. Savannah would never feel alone, never really be alone. He thought about the Sunday he'd spent with her family, aware of the careful scrutiny he had caught each brother giving him.

While he was lost in memories, Savannah stroked his back, feeling the tension seep from his muscles, feeling the change that gradually came over him, until he turned to face her. "Would you believe what you're doing to me?"

"Great day in the morning! What a sexy man!" She melted against him, raising her lips.

It was a lull in their lives that gave them time to devote all their attention to each other. He waited for the trial and received more and more work, which was sent to Savannah's house through the mail. He would spend four or five hours during the day working at the kitchen table, new steel-rimmed glasses perched on his nose, making him look businesslike and at the same time giving Savannah the urge to sit in his lap and pull them off and kiss him.

For several days Savannah left to work at DeVandever's store, but she didn't like being away from Mike, and told them she wouldn't be available to work anymore. She got some projects ready for the fall and caught up on housecleaning she had put off during the year. She knew Mike liked order and neatness, and she made a special effort to organize the clutter, until one afternoon Mike pulled her onto his lap as she passed the table in the kitchen.

"Busy lady, how about a kiss?"

"Mmmm, I might be persuaded," she said, drawing out the words and leaning closer, her tongue touching her lower lip. He leaned down and their tongues met. She sighed and wrapped her arms around his neck, raising her mouth to take his thrusting tongue.

An hour later he shifted her in his arms as they lay stretched out on the living room rug. "I think I was doing something with figures when you walked by—the most delectable figure of all," he said.

"Thank you. I'm glad I outrank columns of twos and threes and fours."

"Of course you do. How could this compare to adding seven plus ten?" he asked, and stroked her breast.

"You keep that up and you won't see any more numbers today."

"Promise?"

She smiled and caught his hands to hold them in hers.

"You were cleaning, weren't you?"

"Yes. I'm glad you could tell."

"I've been meaning to talk to you about that." He

raised up to look down at her, stroking silken strands of hair from her face. "You don't need to neaten up your life or your house for me. I know you like clutter."

She ran her hands through his hair, feeling soft curls wind around her fingers. "I don't have to make it neater, but you like order and you're entitled to some of what you want."

"Why am I entitled?" he asked with an amused glint in his eye.

"Because you're such a stupendous, glorious lover!"

He grinned. "Are you trying to talk me into something?"

"After the past hour? No, of course not!"

He nuzzled her throat, his hand playing lightly across her stomach.

"Mike," she said softly, all teasing gone from her voice.

"You're the best thing that's ever happened to me," he whispered, and she closed her eyes, clinging to his strong shoulders.

Early in July her period came, and disappointment and a sense of desperation shook her. Mike might soon be gone from her life, and she wanted his baby with a longing she hadn't dreamed possible. Deep in her heart she believed that once the trial was out of the way, Mike would view life from a different perspective. She thought he loved her. He was a family man, and deep down she was sure he would change his views on marriage and commitment.

But even if he didn't, she still wanted his baby badly. The first thoughts she had about it were speculative, for she was fearful that she might not be doing the right thing for a baby. But she had kept her appointment with Dr. Borden and discussed her age and single parenting at length with him. And he had pointed out what she had known all along—her family was filled with loving adults and children who would welcome another member with open arms. She had the financial security to be a parent, as well as the time, since teaching gave her a fair amount of freedom. And once she had reasoned out all the arguments and accepted what she wanted to do, she had allowed herself finally to think about becoming a mother, the mother of Mike's child. She knew her love for Mike was greater than any other love she had ever known . . . and she knew it would grow. If only Mike would let down the barriers around his heart. . . .

July passed, and after the first week in August she knew she was pregnant! When the ecstatic realization came, she had to curb the urge to run and tell Mike. He was preoccupied, his thoughts on the coming trial, and she told herself she had to wait and be patient until he could begin to live a normal life again. She calculated the dates, figuring she had become pregnant in the latter part of July. Their baby would be born in the spring!

Their time together was narrowing, and a sense of panic filled her when she held him in her arms, knowing that soon he would leave and he might not come back.

And with each day Mike changed, becoming quieter, more tense and withdrawn.

Finally one afternoon she came home from the grocery store to find him pacing the kitchen. She took one look at the shuttered, angry expression on his face and asked, "What's wrong?"

"Nothing new, except next Tuesday is the nineteenth and the trial begins. I'll move out Monday."

"No! You don't need to do that!"

"They'll hide me in an apartment during the trial."

"Mike," she said, crossing the room swiftly to put her arms around him. She could feel the stiffness in his coiled muscles, see the coldness in his eyes. "Stay here where I can be with you at night. You'll need someone."

His arms went around her and he crushed her to him, kissing her hungrily before he raised his head.

"You're the sweetest person I've ever known," he said huskily. "But I won't endanger your life. I'll stay at the apartment."

"I can't bear for you to be alone through the trial."

He smiled. "You let me unburden my troubles on you, and I never hear so much as a gripe from you about dirty socks in the bathroom."

"That's because I haven't found one single thing, right down to dirty socks, to gripe about. You don't leave dirty socks behind."

"I'm perfect, huh?" he asked with a grin.

"Absolutely! I mean, any man who can do what you can do in bed . . ."

"Like what?" he asked leering.

"Like this," she answered in a seductive drawl as she moved against him, grinding her hips against his.

"Mmmm," he murmured, his hands drifting to her waist. "You don't know what you're talking about, but I love it!" he whispered, then his mouth muffled her answer and all conversation was at an end.

Monday he packed and left, driving her red car to another grocery-store parking lot, where he kissed her good-bye and climbed into a car with his lawyer. Savannah watched them drive away, and a forlorn longing overcame her, like the first drops of water running through a crack in a dam that would soon burst. When she returned to her empty house and faced the fact that Mike might not ever be back, she sank down weakly into a chair. She hurt all over.

Memories assailed her. They had made love on the living-room floor, in the bedroom, on the patio at night. They had danced, eaten, slept in each other's arms, worked, laughed, and talked. And his presence left an aura in the house that tore at her heart.

"Mike, I love you. . . ." she whispered, wanting him so badly, it was painful. She ran her hands over her stomach. She longed for his baby more than she had ever longed for anything in her life, more than she had wanted a child when she had been married to Tyler. She was older now, familiar with children, certain of what she was doing—and more in love than ever before! She felt as if her whole reason for being was to love Mike.

Caught in the dilemma of Mike and his turmoil, she closed her eyes and leaned back in the chair.

The next day was far worse. The morning paper was full of news about the embezzlement scheme, the threats on Mike's life, and reported threats to both the defendants. The statements of Quenton Young hinted that Mike had given false information to the police, that Mike had a part in the fraud, that he was vindictive and determined to ruin an old enemy. She realized there was a strong emotional element in the explosive situation.

With feelings of trepidation she drove downtown. As she walked past the three-tiered fountain on First Street, the city appeared serene, untouched by the stormy trial about to begin.

The Duluth City Complex, which housed the police department, was on her right; the Federal Building, where the trial would be held, to her left. As she climbed the steps past the fountain to the next level on Priley Drive, her gaze lingered on the maples, which would soon be deep red. Ahead stood the fifteen-foot-high statue of a soldier, the stone-and-brick St. Louis County Courthouse directly behind it.

People milled in and out of the buildings, and somewhere inside one of those buildings was Mike. She walked faster, as if by merely being closer to him she could give him moral support. Then she wondered if Mike needed anyone else's support. He seemed self-sufficient, a quality that he had probably developed during childhood after the loss of his parents.

Smoothing her tailored suit, she entered the courtroom and sat in the back. When Mike walked in, she didn't recognize the men who were on either side of him. Mike's gaze swept the spectators. He looked into her eyes without the slightest hint of recognition, and she knew he was doing it to protect her from whoever had threatened him.

His face was flushed with anger, his strong jaw set in a hard line, and his shoulders stiff and tense. Savannah ached so badly for him she wanted to cry. He shouldn't have to go through the trial alone, staying in an apartment without the support and love of family or friends. She thought how lost she would feel in his situation, without her family around to be a buffer against the agony of testifying and the worry about threats.

Her hands were clenched, her nails biting into her flesh, and she didn't hear what was said because she was watching Mike. All she could see was the back of his head, the white shirt collar against his tan neck, the navy suit, which made him look darkly formidable.

During a recess in the trial, Mike left with the two men. As Savannah stood in the crowd milling in the hall, a woman stopped beside her.

"Hi. I haven't seen you in a long time!" she said, smiling broadly.

Smoothing her hair, which was fastened in a chignon, Savannah smiled in return while she wracked her brain for the identity of the woman.

"Can you hold this a second?" the woman asked. "I have a rock in my shoe." She thrust a piece of paper in Savannah's hand.

Savannah glanced down, and her pulse jumped. On the scrap of paper Mike's familiar scrawl read, "Go with Nan. I want to see you."

"Want to come outside where we can talk?" the woman asked.

"Nan?"

She nodded, her brown eyes merry, and Savannah could have hugged her with relief. She listened to Nan's inconsequential chatter as they walked to the stairs and climbed up a flight. As soon as they were alone on the stairs, Nan lowered her voice. "Sorry if I startled you, but we thought this would be safer."

"Thanks. You don't know what it means to me."

Nan arched her brows. "I can guess. Mr. Smith is an unusual man."

Savannah laughed. "Unusual?"

Nan grinned. "I was trying to be polite. He's a hunk!"

"I'll have to agree."

They walked through an outer office, where the two men who had escorted Mike into the courtroom were lounging. Savannah was introduced to them, but two seconds later she couldn't remember their names. All she was aware of was the closed door to her right. Nan opened it, then closed it discreetly as soon as Savannah was inside. Savannah walked straight into Mike's arms, feeling them crush the breath from her lungs as he kissed her deeply.

Their moments together were brief, and that night he phoned and talked to her for three hours. The next day he was called to the stand to testify.

Savannah sat stiff and tense as Mike answered the prosecutor's questions. Then the defense attorney began to tear at his testimony.

Mike was quiet, composed, and positive in his statements, unruffled and sticking to the same facts over and over. Finally he was dismissed and he went back to his seat. His gaze met hers impassively for just a moment before he turned his back and sat down.

She had to see him. Yesterday after the trial he had been whisked to a waiting car, and all she had seen was the back of his head as the car pulled out of the lot.

This time she left early, determined to walk to the car with him, just to touch him and be with him no matter how briefly.

While she stood beneath the shade of a tree, people streamed outside from the courthouse. Sunshine poured warmth over the building and lawn, catching sparkles in the paving, making her squint at the brightness. Suddenly Mike and the two men appeared, hurrying down the steps to avoid reporters. Mike's gaze swept over the area and stopped, meeting hers. She hurried forward, and he said something to the man beside him. The man looked at her, and then she was between them, with Mike hugging her to his side.

"I have to be with you!" she said. "Come home with me! I can't stand knowing you're alone. Please—"

"Okay," he said, interrupting her tumbling flow of words. "We need to ride in their car. Can you leave yours here?"

"Yes!" she said with enormous relief.

They reached the long black car, and one of the men opened the door. Suddenly a shot rang out, blasting the quiet afternoon and sending a stab of ice through Savannah.

Seven

Mike gasped and swore, shoving Savannah into the backseat of the car and falling in after her as the window shattered. Glass sprinkled over them, bits falling on the dark seat in front of her face. When the men were inside, the car moved away in seconds, and they were racing down the street while pandemonium broke out behind them. Mike lifted his weight off Savannah and pulled her up beside him.

"Are you all right?" she asked.

He swore steadily in a low voice. His hands were clenched, and spots of anger burned his cheeks a deep red.

One of the men in the front was talking on a phone while they drove.

"Mike, come home," she urged. "Let's go home instead of to the apartment."

"We can't. I have to have bodyguards, protection. You saw what happened back there—you should avoid me."

"No!" she said, clutching his arm tightly, determined to stay with him.

For an instant some of the harshness left his features. His eyes lost their glacial ice and he stroked her cheek lightly with his knuckles. "Savannah," he said softly. "I should send you packing for your own safety, but I can't. Do you want to come with me?"

"Of course," she answered, touching his fist. She laced her fingers in his as he relaxed. He pulled her close beside him and they didn't say a word until they were at the apartment. While he talked to the two men she looked around, barely noticing the white and wine-red decor, the thick off-white carpet, and floor-to-ceiling windows that looked out on a swimming pool. When the men left them, Mike shut and locked the door, then turned to her.

She hurt when she saw the stormy anger and frustration in his eyes. She wrapped her arms around him, and his own arms tightened about her like iron fetters, as if he could pull all her warmth and joy into his soul by holding her close.

"Thank heaven you're here!" He ground out the words, his breath fanning over her ear. Then he swept her into his arms and carried her to the bedroom, kicking the door shut behind them.

Later they learned the police had apprehended a hired gunman who said a man named John Jones had paid him to kill Mike, but the information stopped there. The lawmen couldn't trace the shooting to either O'Toole or Young.

Savannah stayed at the apartment the next night, riding to the trial with Mike, returning with him, letting her family pick up her car and lock up her house.

She was eager to see Dr. Borden, but she knew she had to wait until the trial was over. And she prayed with all her heart that when the trial *was* finished, Mike would relax and rethink his views on life.

He was so tense with anger and bitterness now that she often felt as if she were with a ruthless stranger. His lovemaking held a desperate need, an urgency that made him rough and demanding, yet exciting, never too forceful. She met his passion with an unbridled abandon, loving him with every ounce of her being.

During Zack O'Toole's testimony, there were moments when Savannah had decided that he was the one who had threatened Mike and hired the killers, but then when Quenton Young testified, her opinion swayed and she was convinced that it had been Young. His hatred of Mike oozed from every look he gave him and from his testimony, until Savannah became fearful Mike would be indicted and an investigation would be made to see if he had taken any of the money.

On the fourth day of the trial, O'Toole and Young were convicted and it was over. As the sentence was read and the gavel banged down, Mike clenched his fists, pent-up fury rippling through him like stormy waves. Quenton had done his best to discredit Mike, and Mike was convinced it was he who had hired the killers. From the front of the courtroom Quenton turned, his pale blue eyes meeting Mike's.

Mike felt the flare of hatred from Quenton and the hot rush of his own anger. His fists tightened. How he would like an hour alone with that man! Because of him he had to leave his home, Savannah, his job; Brian had been threatened. Fury made Mike shake as he fought to control the urge to cross the narrow space between them and slug Quenton.

Quenton's face paled suddenly as he watched Mike, and he turned away swiftly, whispering something to the guard, who glanced at Mike and stepped between them. Mike turned his back on them.

It's over, he kept reassuring himself as he sought Savannah, spotting her golden hair quickly. She glanced at him and away, showing no more recognition now than at any other time in the courtroom. He watched her turn and leave, her hips moving slightly with the sway he found so provocative. He felt an arousal that made him want to stride down the aisle, scoop her into his arms, and carry her home to bed. He rubbed his jaw. *It's over and I move now. I tell Savannah good-bye.*

The thought hurt, but he had the threads of his life to try to pick up, and he knew Savannah would never leave her family and the life she had established in Duluth. And logically he knew he shouldn't urge her to leave. But she had become part of his life; she had renewed him in a way he hadn't thought would ever be possible. He loved now. . . .

The ache he felt when he thought of parting from her was interwoven with the hurts and regrets over leaving Duluth, leaving the house that had been his home for the past twenty years, leaving all that was important to him. He squared his shoulders and stepped outside.

Savannah stood in the shade of a maple tree. She was waiting, sunlight making a golden halo of her hair. His gaze traveled swiftly down her body, his imagination peeling away her navy cotton dress, seeing her in the pale pink lacy bra she sometimes wore, the thin, brief bikini panties that hugged her flesh.

He hated the thought of parting with her, but he had known the moment was coming when they would each have to go separate ways. In the meantime . . . His pulse jumped as he thought about undressing her and watching her green eyes darken with desire.

He drew a sharp breath and glanced around, suddenly aware of danger. If he had been fantasizing the way he was now on the day they had shot at him, he probably would be in a hospital. Or worse. His gaze swept the street, the sidewalk, and the mingling crowd, and he realized he shouldn't make contact with Savannah and draw her into danger. Vaguely he wondered if he would really be safe in New Mexico. Worries plagued him, doubts and concerns, and his anger raged inside him. He saw a reporter heading toward him and he turned away, knowing his attorney would field the questions.

His fingers closed on Savannah's arm, and they rushed to the waiting car. The door slammed and the car started along Priley Drive. Seconds ticked past, the time he had to be with Savannah dwindling. With a groan of frustration he pulled her onto his lap, aware that he was handling her roughly. Yet his emotions were so turbulent, he couldn't help it. His fingers shook as they tangled in her hair, sending her hairpins tumbling while he silenced her protest completely with his mouth.

At the apartment they locked the door and were alone. Mike faced her as he pulled off his suit coat and dropped it over the back of a chair.

"It's over," he said. "This is my last night here. The house has been sold, the furniture temporarily moved to storage. At eleven tonight I go to the airport and fly to Santa Fe, and they've warned me not to come back for a long, long time."

She listened in silence, wanting him, loving him. He pulled off his tie, his gaze raking down over her straight-lined dress, with its simple white collar and narrow ribbon tie. "Will you come see me in Santa Fe?" he asked, crossing the room to slip his arms around her waist.

"How soon do you want me?"

"Next weekend, the last weekend in August."

"Okay. I have to start back at school next Tuesday, but I can come after school on Friday."

"And after the semester starts you won't have as much time to come to Santa Fe," he said flatly, knowing what was inevitable, but determined to put it out of his mind for now.

"I can come on weekends whenever you want me."

"I want you," he said, grinding out the words.

Savannah was crushed to his hard chest. His kisses were hot and demanding, and she realized something was changing forever between them. The idyll was over. They would either go on to a lasting commitment—or part forever.

She held him tightly, her arms wrapped around his neck. She ached to tell him about the baby, but knew she couldn't trap Mike into marriage.

"Savannah, I've given you my address and phone number. I'll go by the name Mike Williams in Santa Fe. The police here think Quenton and Zack may be linked with organized crime mobsters, so they've warned me to be cautious." He framed her face with his strong fingers. "Honey, I don't want to put you in the slightest danger. You don't have to come—"

Oblivious to her hot tears, she stood on tiptoe to kiss him and halt his words. He groaned, locking his arms around her. He held her so tightly, she thought she might faint, and his ravenous kisses stirred her to a frenzy of passion.

"Mike, I hate the fact that you have to go, when I know you don't want to move," she whispered. "You'll get along. I know you—"

His mouth stopped her words now, and all thought evaporated like dew under a summer sun. The sense of urgency Mike had shown during the days of the trial was as strong as ever. His hands freed the back of her navy dress and pulled it down off her shoulders. He yanked away his own clothing, peeled off her lacy underwear in haste, then scooped her into his arms to carry her to bed.

He was so handsome, she thought, his coppery body muscular, his stomach flat, his maleness throbbing for her.

"You're beautiful," he whispered, and bent his dark head over her, kissing her above her knees, making her shift her hips and moan softly. Her fingers wound through his hair as his hands roamed freely, caressing in an onslaught that aroused her clamoring senses.

Finally she gasped, pulling at his shoulders. "Mike, please . . . take me . . ."

He moved over her, raising her hips with his hands, and entered her slowly, causing her body to arch in sweet agony and a moan to escape her lips.

In seconds they were moving together, and Mike whispered her name over and over until finally he groaned and cried out, shuddering with release, complete with her in a union that Savannah felt to her soul.

While he held her in his arms and they talked, Mike's watch ticked the minutes away. The time came when they had to shower and dress and leave for the airport.

The lawmen had given him a disguise, including a wig, along with new identity papers. Savannah kissed him good-bye, and then he was on his own. The men took a winding route when the drove her home, to make sure they weren't being followed.

She entered her dark, empty house. She was alone, aware that Mike was flying to New Mexico that very second, conscious of the time and distance that would separate them now, and also stingingly aware that Mike could make his new life complete without her.

Her hands went to her stomach and she smiled, the first of the tears she had been holding back spilling over her cheeks. She had his baby. Forever. Part of Mike and his love, a child she had wanted so intensely.

The next morning she made an appointment to see Dr. Borden on the following Wednesday afternoon after school.

She sat across his desk from him while he rubbed the bridge of his nose and gazed at her with friendly brown eyes. A lock of brown hair curled on his forehead, and he pushed it away impatiently, then picked up a slip of paper from his desk. He held it out to her.

"Here's what I want you to take—some iron tablets. You're slightly anemic. Have you told the father-to-be yet, Savannah?"

"If the baby isn't due until the end of April or first of May, I have lots of time," she said, and he smiled.

"You'll handle it just fine, the way you do everything else. You look so radiant. . . ." His voice trailed off, and he shrugged. "Any questions?"

"No, and thank you."

He pulled a ledger in front of him to write something down. "I'll see you in a month."

"Thanks," she said. She left his office and stopped to pay the bill at the front desk. She hummed softly, feeling a bond that bridged the distance to Mike, and she couldn't resist the temptation to stop in a baby shop and buy a musical stuffed bear.

Since it had been confirmed that she was pregnant, she called her sister Ginny and went to see her after school on Thursday.

While Ginny made a tossed salad, Savannah tried to think of how to open the conversation. There didn't seem to be any roundabout way to lead into it. "Ginny, I want to talk to you about something personal."

Ginny turned wide green eyes on Savannah, her auburn brows arching in question. At that moment the back door opened and quickly slammed shut, and Monty came bounding into the kitchen, his five-year-old voice high and filled with excitement. "Kenny's mom said she would take us all to get a milk shake if you said okay! Can I go?"

Ginny glanced at the clock. "Almost two hours until dinner. Okay." She dried her hands while Monty followed her hopefully to her purse.

"Jill wants to go too," he said. "And Ted wants to go."

"And the whole neighborhood?" Ginny asked. He grinned while she fished out some change and dropped it into his hand. "Are you sure she wants to take all of you?"

"Yes! She said she wants us and she said she wanted Jill."

"Okay, okay. Be sure to thank her."

"We will!" He ran for the door.

"Hey, what do you say?"

He yelled, "Thanks!" and the door slammed behind him. Pushing up the sleeves of her green sweater, Ginny walked over to the table. She pulled out a chair and sat down across from Savannah. "What's on your mind?"

"I'm pregnant."

Ginny's eyes widened, and for an instant her mouth was a round O. Then she smiled. "I'm so happy for you! Oh, Savannah, how wonderful! Mike is just great! The whole family loved him. That is the most wonderful news." She reached across the table to give her sister a squeeze, and for a moment Savannah's eyes misted over.

Her throat ached, and she fought back tears of

joy. How wonderful it was to tell someone, to have someone share her elation!

Ginny smiled at her, and Savannah grinned back. "I should've taken one look at you and guessed," Ginny said quietly. "That is the most wonderful news I've had in years. Have you told Mom and Dad?"

"Not yet. You're the first. Dr. Borden excepted."

"And Mike!" Ginny laughed. "Oh, how great! When's the wedding?"

Savannah's jubilation diminished. "There isn't one planned yet."

"Well, my goodness, you'd better get to it! Babies don't wa—" Ginny bit off her words. "You and Mike do plan to marry, don't you?"

"Not at this point. Remember, Ginny, he's had the trial to face, the threats and attempts on his life, moving, getting a new job . . . Marriage isn't what he's thinking about."

"Are you?" Ginny asked flatly.

Savannah pinched the bridge of her nose as she thought over how to answer Ginny. "I think when his life settles down, he may want to marry."

"Aren't you going to tell him you're pregnant?"

Savannah shook her head. "I might not. Mike's gone now, and he told me from the start he wouldn't marry again."

"Savannah!" Ginny stared at her, shock widening her eyes. "You can't mean that."

"I do," Savannah said, wrapped in protective layers of calm that came from the full knowledge of what she wanted.

"Well, you have three brothers who can have a talk with Mr. Michael Jefferson Smith!"

"No! I knew what I was doing, and this is the way I want it. I don't want Mike to know because I don't want another divorce. He would marry me instantly if he knew about my pregnancy. But he would do it out of a sense of duty. Ginny, I didn't confide in you to have you tell Mike! Promise me you'll leave all that to me."

"I think you're making a mistake," Ginny said, her brow furrowed. "He seemed so in love with you. I saw him watching you all the time. He didn't want you out of his sight."

"Well, I'm out of it now, and his feelings have stayed the same. But he may change eventually. This is the first time we've been separated since we met, and he's had the problems of the world on his shoulders." She traced a circle on the table with her finger. "I hope he'll want to marry, because I love him with all my heart."

"Then for heaven's sake tell him!"

"No! I don't want to trap him into marriage, and don't you see—that's what I'd be doing."

"So if he doesn't ask you to marry, you'll have this baby alone?"

Savannah smiled, and asked gently, "How alone will I be? I have you and Brit and Paris and Pete and Ray and Mom and Dad and—"

"Okay, okay." Ginny ran her hands nervously over her apron. "But he seemed to love you. . . ."

"And if he really does, sooner or later he'll want to marry."

"Have you ever thought about marrying and then falling in love? It does happen."

"I'm already in love and I know Mike loves me to a degree."

"Oh, brother!"

"Well, he does, but he doesn't want another marriage, and if his feelings don't change, I won't force him into it out of a misguided notion of duty!"

"Did it ever occur to you that he might resent not knowing about his baby?"

"Yes, but he's a grown man who has said he never wants to marry again. He's made his choices, just as I made mine."

"Savannah, listen to the voice of experience. Children are an enormous responsibility—financial, emotional, physical, moral—in every way."

"I'm aware of that, and you know how badly I've wanted a baby. Ginny, as much as I love children and have wanted a baby, I want this one a hundred times more because he will be part of Mike."

"And you're already calling it *he*, huh? You are so damned naive and trusting!"

"I know what I want. And I know this child will come into a big family filled with love for him."

"Yeah, but his mother deserves something better."

Savannah shrugged. "Things will sort themselves out, and I'll always have our child. Oh, Ginny, you don't know how badly I want this ba—" She started to cry, unable to say another word.

"Hey, Savannah, don't cry. You do have all of us. And if you ever want to tell Mike, you know any of us will do it for you."

"No!" she said, wiping her eyes swiftly with the back of her hand, shocked at her loss of control. "You have to promise me you won't tell him, and you have to promise to help make the others see why. I'm just so happy, Ginny! So long ago all my dreams about family and children died with Tyler. I gave up, and never thought I would have a baby. I talked to Dr. Borden about this before I got pregnant."

"You did it deliberately!" Ginny said softly, staring at her sister.

"Of course. I love Mike, and here was a chance to keep some part of him forever and to have the baby I've always wanted. Mike's son."

"You're crazy, but you know we'll do anything you want. And we'll love the baby."

"Dr. Borden said this baby will have grandparents and twelve fathers and eleven mothers, if he counted all the Blair kids correctly," Savannah said with a smile.

"Well, I guess he's right," Ginny agreed. "All your nieces and nephews will adore having another baby in the family. Our Jill is three now, and the youngest in the family. Nothing would please her more than a baby, and unfortunately we can't oblige. If we can see to it that our three children are educated and grow up healthy, we'll be doing the best we can."

"I don't want to tell anyone else for a while."

"Tell Mom."

"I will. I meant the others and the children."

"That's going to be awkward, Savannah, but children will accept anything. And they know Mike. I can't resist saying it one more time. Tell Mike."

"Not yet. I've got to give him time to get settled and get his life straightened out. Then I hope he'll want me and the same things I want, but if he doesn't I won't hold him by using the baby."

"You're absolutely crazy. I know he loves you."

"He may love his independence more." She stood up. "I have to run. I'm flying to Santa Fe this weekend."

"You take care of yourself. Do you feel okay?"

"I feel grand most of the time."

Ginny studied her a moment. "You look . . . glowing. I should've guessed, but I thought it was just Mike who caused the glow."

"He did cause it!"

"You know what I mean. I'll bet Mom has noticed."

"Maybe so. I'll talk to her tomorrow."

Ginny hugged her sister. "If you need anything, give a call."

"I will. I promise."

"And think about telling Mike. He may not have as strong a sense of duty as you think."

"Sure."

Savannah got home in time to answer her ringing phone. Mike's voice came through loud and sure, and she sank down on the sofa, feeling happy. As they talked, she was relieved to hear that Mike liked Santa Fe. His enthusiasm was unmistakable as he talked about the town and its history and culture. And more important, he wanted to show it all to her.

Eight

On Friday Savannah flew to Santa Fe and Mike met her at the airport.

He spotted her as she emerged from the ramp of the plane. Savannah's gaze swept over the crowd, and her long golden hair swayed slightly with each step she took. She had let it fall free, the silky strands cascading down over her shoulders and back. Mike's heart seemed to stop, then start again at a faster tempo as he stared at her. He loved her and had missed her terribly, and was amazed at the intensity of his reaction at seeing her again. He wanted to keep her with him, but he had to remind himself that she had a complete, happy life and family still in Duluth. And he knew full well how terrible it was to be uprooted from family, home, and friends.

When her gaze locked with his, his pulse underwent another jolt. Without hesitation she walked into his waiting arms, and he bent his head to kiss her. Her lips were soft, her breath sweet, and for an instant he thrust his tongue into the velvety softness of her mouth. Instantly a rush of heated desire buffeted him, so he released her.

"Welcome to Santa Fe," he said gruffly, wanting to scoop her into his arms and crush her against him.

Her eyes sparkled and her dimple appeared. "The Chamber of Commerce should hire you to greet every arrival!"

"No, thank you! Only one very special person gets that greeting!" he said, drinking in the sight of her, thinking she was even more lovely than the last time he had seen her. She seemed to sparkle. Her eyes were shining, her cheeks were flushed, and he forgot he was simply standing and staring at her.

"That's good news," she replied cheerfully.

"I can't wait to get you home!" he said, and the words enticed her like cellophane-wrapped bonbons.

As they left and stepped outside, the warm evening reminded her of the summer nights they'd spent together.

"Mike, it's summer here!" she exclaimed, inhaling deeply and relishing the night air.

"Honey, Santa Fe is great! You're going to love it, and I can't wait to show it to you. Look at me—I'm turning into a Santa Fean." He held up his foot, and she saw his new western boots. And he wore a wide leather belt with a silver buckle. He looked as marvelous to her as he had in sneakers and cut-offs.

"Very handsome!"

He grinned and took her hands. Under a yellow light in the parking lot, he turned her to face him. While he held her hands locked in his warm ones, his gaze drifted down over her navy skirt and pale blue short-sleeved sweater. Then he looked into her eyes. "How good it is to have you here!"

Her heart jumped, and she walked into his arms to kiss him again.

"Let's go," he whispered moments later, and she nodded. Her heart beat with joy because she felt to her soul that Mike was getting over the stress of the trial. And he seemed so glad to see her.

As he held open the car door for her, she noticed him watchfully studying the area, and a cold fear struck her. The moment he was behind the wheel she asked, "Have you been safe?"

"Yes," he said abruptly.

"I saw you look all around. Is everything okay here?"

"Yes, so far. I just find it difficult to let down my guard."

"Oh, Mike, thank goodness!" she exclaimed, closing her eyes as she expelled her breath in relief.

"I didn't mean to worry you!" he said sharply. Then he sighed, and his voice changed. "It's hard to forget."

"I just want it to be safe for you here. I want you to be able to live a normal life."

"I will—now that you're here."

The last vestige of her fear fled, and she scooted closer to him.

"I didn't tell you when we talked on the phone," he said, "because I didn't know his schedule, but Brian is home for a weekend before he goes back to college in California."

"I'll get to meet him," she said, suddenly wondering if Mike's son would like her.

"Don't sound worried. You'll like him."

"I wasn't worried about my liking *him*!"

"He'll adore you. He's a good kid. You'll see."

"Just like his dad."

Mike grinned and pulled her closer. "We won't have as much privacy, but I'm glad you two are going to get to know each other."

"I am too," she said with sincerity. "Tell me about your new job." While she listened she wanted to touch Mike, to kiss him, to be held in his arms, and she barely noticed the scenery. She wanted to be loved and held, to love Mike in return, but even more compelling was the joyous urge to share the news of her pregnancy with him. Yet she had to wait! Streetlights shone on adobe houses, tall cottonwoods, and wide streets, but it was all a dim blur, because her attention was elsewhere. She couldn't resist trailing her hand across the nape of Mike's neck and weaving her fingers through his hair. His voice faded as he glanced at her. "How do you expect me to talk to you?"

"I'm disturbing you?" She looked into his eyes and felt a flame burst into searing brightness within her. "Now you're disturbing me," she whispered hoarsely.

"I'm just thinking about you," he said, shifting his attention back to driving as he turned the car onto Upper Canyon Road. "Until we get home, in the interests of safety and sane driving you'd better stop what you're doing," he added dryly.

"And you take your hand off my knee," she retorted as she scooted away.

"That's not interfering with anything."

"That's what you think!"

"I'll show you downtown Santa Fe tomorrow. Right now I want to take you home with me."

"Whatever suits you," she said, turning to study him, to drink in the sight of his muscular legs and arms, to glimpse his furred chest where his cotton shirt gaped open slightly at the neck.

They turned into a curving gravel drive, and she shifted in her seat to look at a sprawling house of beige stuccoed adobe that looked far too big for Mike. It was solid, the type of home for a family, with a two-car garage and an expanse of dark, sloping lawn.

"You have a big house," she said softly, her pulse skipping in the hope that he had purchased it with a family in mind.

"I want to feel as if I belong somewhere, as if I'm permanent," he said roughly. The old note of anger in his tone flared briefly, but when he opened her door for her the anger was gone. Outside lights illuminated the area around the house. A blue Ford was parked in the drive, and she felt an unusual flutter of nervousness over the prospect of meeting Brian.

She paused a moment to look at the house. "It's lovely, Mike," she said, feeling momentarily overwhelmed. She hadn't imagined his house would be quite so large.

"Thanks. I hoped you'd like it. Come inside." They entered a back hallway lined with coatracks and clothing hooks. Next was a big, rustic kitchen with a gray stone beehive fireplace, modern appliances, wood cabinets, and a fuzzy collie that ambled over to greet them.

"That's Pirate, Brian's dog, who gets shuffled around among Brian's friends."

"Hi," a deep voice said from the doorway, and Savannah looked up.

With a sense of shock she saw what Mike must have looked like at twenty. Brian had his father's features. He had the same thickly lashed blue eyes, but a more slender frame and a less formidable, more sunny appearance, with unruly brown hair and dimples in his cheeks.

"Savannah, this is my son, Brian."

"I never would've guessed!" she said with a smile, extending her hand.

Brian took it in his large hand without hesitation as his father said, "Brian, meet Mrs. Carson."

"Oh, please, just call me Savannah!"

"Sure. Dad's told me about you. Why don't I take Savannah's suitcase to her room?"

"Okay," Mike said, handing it to Brian. With Pirate trailing at his heels, Brian disappeared into the hall, and Savannah turned to Mike.

"He's the image of you!"

"Minus several pounds and gray hair and wrinkles and grumpy disposition . . ."

"What an ogre I've fallen in love with!"

"Ahh, that sounds good," he said. He pulled her to him, leaning down to kiss her, but she stepped away.

"Mike! Brian will be right back."

"He knows I love you and he knows men and women kiss."

Her laughter was lost in his kiss, and she clung to him for seconds, then pushed away. "He may know all that, but don't embarrass me!"

"Come see the house, and we'll have a drink and talk." His voice dropped. "That wasn't what I had originally scheduled."

She gave him a smile, and moved ahead of him. She didn't want Brian to come back and find her kissing Mike, oblivious to everything else. She wanted to get to know Brian, to ease into a relationship that she hoped would be important.

Brian met them in the hall, and Mike said, "I'm going to show Savannah the house. Why don't you pour Savannah and me some white wine and get something for yourself?"

"Sure, Dad."

Savannah had never seen Mike's house in Duluth or his furniture, and her curiosity was growing swiftly. They went down two steps into a living room that had white stuccoed walls and heavy dark timbers across the ceiling. A grand piano, a television, stereo, and big, comfortable beige furniture filled the room, but the instant Savannah saw it she knew why the interior of the *Bluebell* had disturbed Mike so deeply. To her the room resembled a house half-furnished, awaiting an occupant. Tables were polished and lovely, but bare. It was Spartan and immaculate, and Savannah felt she wouldn't be able to exist in its austere simplicity.

"There isn't any new furniture," Mike said. "It's all from my house in Duluth." That made matters worse, because for a fleeting moment she had hoped he hadn't settled in yet, that he was still in the process of furnishing the house.

"What's wrong?" he asked mildly.

Startled that her feelings had shown, she said, "You and I are opposites in more ways than one. No wonder the *Bluebell* bothered you. You're so . . . neat!"

"Don't make it sound sinful!"

"I'm not sure I'll fit in—even for a weekend."

"You'll fit," he said. "I love you even if you are a mess," he added teasingly, but she wondered how long it would be before her casual attitude would begin to grate on him.

One picture hung on the wall, and she walked over to it to look at it more closely. It was of an Indian woman, and the signature in the corner read R. C. Gorman.

"This is really nice, Mike."

"That's my one new purchase. Gorman's a Taos artist. Come see the rest of the house," he said, pausing at the first door off a long hallway. "This will be your room." He ushered her into a beige-and-white room with a mahogany four-poster bed. It was plainer than the living room, but a bouquet of red roses on the dresser caught her attention immediately. She crossed the room to read the card.

"I missed you," was all it said, but as she turned back to Mike, she felt a tight lump in her throat. She wanted badly to share the news about the baby with him! All of his actions since the moment she had stepped off the plane indicated he loved her deeply. The big home needed a family, not one bachelor living alone.

"It was mutual," she whispered, putting her arms around his neck and inhaling his familiar, woodsy scent. "They're lovely. Thank you."

His arms tightened around her, and he moved backward slightly to shove the door closed with his foot. She felt as if she might drown in his eyes as he studied her hungrily, and she waited, holding her breath for a declaration of love, expecting one any moment.

"I'm beginning to wish you and Brian could meet another time," he whispered. Then his lips brushed hers and her thoughts vanished. She ran her hands across his hard shoulders, pressing against him as she let her feelings show in her response.

His arousal was swift, and she stepped back. "Mike, this won't do! You'll embarrass both of us in front of your son."

The fires in his eyes revealed a blatant male need that made her tremble. She left the room quickly. His bedroom was next, and it, too, was neat and plain. It had a wide-screen television and a king-sized bed that held her attention so long, he couldn't help but notice.

"I want you there with me," he said softly, the words a scalding touch on her senses.

She drew a sharp breath and felt a flush of embarrassment on her cheeks. "I don't know how you do it!"

He raised an eyebrow, a quizzical smile on his face. "Do what, love?"

The endearment sent a shiver of pleasure coursing through her. "Make me blush. I haven't blushed in years! Now suddenly I'm . . ." Her voice trailed off as a sense of longing tugged at her.

"In love, maybe?" he asked with a smile.

"Very much," she said solemnly, unable to smile in return. She wanted so badly to tell him about their baby, to have him declare lasting love, and to ask her to share his home and life—the things that were constantly in her thoughts.

"If you won't let me lock the door and make love to you, shall we join Brian?"

"Fine. That's best."

She caught a flicker of curiosity in Mike's eyes, but she moved past him quickly before he could question her, and she hoped nothing showed in her expression. He had a knack for discerning her emotions as plainly as if she had a sign around her neck describing how she felt.

Brian stood as soon as they entered the large family room. This room sported navy leather furniture, a square Navajo rug, and another wide-screen television. An unnecessary fire burned in the fireplace, sending an enticing smell of piñon into the room. Brian held out a glass of wine, which Savannah took from him before sitting down.

"While you two get acquainted, I'm going to see about dinner," Mike said, and left the room.

"How was your trip?" she asked, and for the next half hour while she idly scratched Pirate's head as he sat at her knee, she listened to Brian talk about his overseas adventures. When Mike called them to the kitchen, they sat down to eat grilled steaks, green beans, and baked potatoes.

As Brian buttered his steaming potato, he smiled at her. "I hear you rammed and sank Dad's boat, and your first meeting was sort of explosive."

She looked quickly at Mike, who smiled and held out a serving bowl.

"Care for some homegrown tomatoes?" he asked.

"Since when have you had time to grow tomatoes?" she asked.

"I'll have to admit they came with the house."

"And will you please tell your son what actually happened during the storm on the lake?"

Mike's eyes became round, but the devilish twinkle gave him away.

"Dad?" Brian asked, his dimples showing as his brows arched in curiosity.

"I told it right. The *Bluebell* hit the *Marietta* and down went my boat! And I was lucky to crawl out of the lake and survive!"

"That isn't so," she said firmly, knowing Mike was enjoying teasing her. "It was just the opposite, Brian. Your father rammed my houseboat, and the jolt almost threw me into the lake." She turned to Mike. "And I pulled you out of the lake!"

"No, you didn't! Brian, you see the difficulties I've had with this woman."

Brian laughed, his eyes sparkling with merriment. "Yeah, Dad, I do see! She rammed you like the time you told Mom I drove over her petunias!" He turned to Savannah. "For a brave man who'll take on a fight, my dad has moments when he's a real chicken."

"Petunias?" Savannah asked, amused to see Mike's cheeks turn red.

"That was a long time ago," he muttered. "You haven't said a word about my tomatoes."

"I want to hear about the petunias. He drove over a flower bed?"

"No," Brian said cheerfully. "Mom bought some new petunias and left them in little cardboard boxes on the drive, and Dad didn't see them. But I got the blame."

"That's because your mother would be more tolerant about your driving over them!"

They all laughed, and while Brian cut into his thick steak he asked, "I suppose the story that you threatened Dad with an ax was another of his yarns?"

This time Savannah blushed. "Actually, no, but he did slug me first."

Brian's eyes widened, and he paused with his fork in midair. "You *hit* her?"

"I thought she was a man," Mike said, his warm gaze catching and holding Savannah's. In that moment it was as if they were alone. A bond of silent communication enveloped them, shutting out the world. She knew Mike was remembering, just as she was.

While Mike's attention was snared by her green eyes, images danced in his mind of Savannah standing in the rain with the soggy hat and the ax, ready to battle him. The vision transformed, with fiery alchemy, to the first breathtaking moment when he had peeled away her clothing. As he watched her, he saw a flicker of response in her expression. Tension sparked between them, a silent message of mutual longing conveyed only by eyes, but as unmistakable as sunshine.

When Savannah pulled her gaze from Mike's, she realized Brian had lowered his fork to his plate and was staring at them with curiosity. Embarrassed, she changed the subject. "Your tomatoes are delicious. What else are you growing?"

With an amused arch of his eyebrow, Mike answered, and she wondered why a simple response about his garden could make her feel tingly. Another glance into his eyes gave her the reason. She realized the expression she saw was love. But, then, why wouldn't he acknowledge his feelings?

Brian and Mike talked about the yard and house, and she pursued her question in her thoughts. She reminded herself that Mike might have no intention of marrying again no matter how he felt toward her. Every time she came up against that possibility, she felt a tight knot of pain. She looked up to find him watching her as he sipped his water.

"Right, Savannah?"

She went blank. She hadn't heard a word he had said. "I'm sorry. I was lost in thought about how you cooked the beans."

Amusement flared in his eyes again, this time making her blush, and she kept her attention on the conversation through the rest of the meal.

After dinner Brian and Mike insisted on cleaning up. Then two of Brian's friends appeared, and all of them played a trivia game.

At ten o'clock Brian and his friends left for a late movie. As soon as Mike locked the door behind them, he moved around the room turning off lights until he reached Savannah. She was putting away the game when he grabbed her.

"Alone at last!"

She smiled as his arms wrapped around her. "You have a marvelous son."

"Thank you. I think so too." His blue eyes darkened and his embrace tightened. "It's been so damned long," he said gruffly, and dipped his head, his lips meeting hers, his tongue thrusting into her mouth. He kissed her deeply, his tongue savoring her as he molded her body to his. His muscled thighs pressed against her while his strong arms kept her from falling.

She felt dizzy, on fire with need. She was only dimly aware of what was going on as he swung her into his arms and continued to kiss her. Silently he carried her to his room, where he placed her carefully on the bed.

She sat up to tug at his belt buckle, feeling the coarse denim against her knuckles, his hands on her sweater. He slipped the sweater over her head and tossed it aside, then knelt to cup her breast in his large, callused hand. His flesh was dark brown against her paleness. His fingers pushed away the last bit of lace covering her breasts and his thumb flicked over a trembling bud.

She gasped, closing her eyes as she leaned forward to slide his shirt off his shoulders. She trailed light kisses down his throat. "Mike, please," she whispered, feeling an urgency that made her ache. She adored him, and physical love was the expression of her heart's desire.

He pushed her down gently, watching her as he undressed. Keys jingled when his jeans hit the floor. She twisted on her side to run her fingers in the tight waistband of his navy briefs and tug them down, releasing him from their constriction. Her fingers trailed over his legs, feeling the short, dark hairs, the sinewy muscles, and the ridges from his scars. Then her hands drifted across his stomach, and he groaned. He lay down on the bed and pulled her against him as he kissed her.

Savannah wrapped her arms around his neck as her hips ground against his maleness and sensations rocked her, longing bursting into white-hot flames.

Finally she cried out, moving beneath him, "Mike, now . . . I want you!"

"Savannah, love . . ."

He lowered his weight, thrusting into her welcoming warmth. She gave to him with her body and soul, their joining going beyond the physical as she whispered over and over, "I love you. . . ."

Later she lay in Mike's arms while they talked about a hundred topics, but none involved their future together. She was alternately caught between an overwhelming joy in touching him and a tight constriction that it was all she would ever have of him.

Long after Mike slept she lay in his arms staring at his profile in the darkened room. "I love you," she whispered, wanting desperately to have him return her love fully. She moved his arm so that his relaxed hand lay on her stomach, over their baby. She placed her hand lightly on his, holding it against her, wishing more than she had ever wanted anything before to be able to share with Mike the news of their child.

In time she slipped out of his arms, gathered her things, and tiptoed to her room. Exhaustion filled her, erasing her worries as she fell asleep.

The next morning when she left her room, Mike greeted her as he came from the kitchen. He had on a short-sleeved western shirt, tight, faded jeans, and his boots. The warmth of his gaze made her tingle as she walked to him and he slipped his arm around her waist. "I want to show you something," he said.

They walked outside onto a covered patio, where a table with a bouquet of flowers in the center was set for breakfast for three. Pirate raised his head to look at them, then lay back down on the uneven tiles.

Savannah took everything in at a glance, but what held her gaze were the mountains. The sky was as clear and blue as Mike's eyes, and the mountains were a vivid green. "It's gorgeous!"

"I know. I love to sit out here. You're looking at the Sangre de Cristo Mountains. And next month, the first two weeks of October, the aspen will turn yellow. I want you to see them with me."

"I want to," she replied softly, wondering if he would go on, but Brian came outside with a cheerful greeting and glasses of orange juice, and the moment was gone.

Brian left after breakfast, and Mike drove Savannah to town. He parked at the La Fonda hotel. As he draped his arm across her shoulders he said, "La Fonda is Spanish for the end, and this is where the Santa Fe Trail ended. We need to walk to really appreciate Santa Fe. Come on, I'll give you the deluxe tour."

She matched her stride to his, thinking how handsome he looked as sunlight caught dark glints in his hair. He told her about the Plaza, the town square with the hotel on one side and the Palace of the Governors on the other.

She looked at adobe buildings containing galleries and shops. "I know how you collect things," he said as he held open the door to a curio shop. "Get what you want and don't argue, or I'll pick out something."

"Mike, that isn't necessary."

He shrugged. "Okay, Savannah. I warned you." He walked around all the counters and finally purchased a pink-and-lime plaster ashtray in the shape of a smiling donkey with bold black letters across its side reading, "Greetings from New Mexico."

He handed the gift to her, and she laughed and kissed him. "Now, what shall we get next?" he asked.

"I'll find something! I like the silver bracelets. The *plain* silver bracelets."

"Okay. And what else?"

She selected a simple silver bracelet, a vase of deep-blue glass, a pottery bowl, and paper flowers.

As they left a third shop, Mike asked, "Want to help me with something?"

His expression was bland, giving no clue to what his question was about. "Sure," she answered.

"Good. I need a painting to hang over the mantel. Pick one out for me."

"I'll be glad to, but I don't know anything about artists."

"The galleries we'll visit will have good artists. No problem there."

"You might not like what I choose. We're opposites when it comes to decor."

"Not necessarily. I'll tell you if I don't like it, but I want you to select one. When I look at it, I'll know you picked it out."

How could she argue with that? She nodded. "Fine. You'd better tell me the price range."

"I don't want you to look at the price. I'll worry about the cost."

She stopped abruptly to stare at him. The corner of his mouth raised in a crooked grin. "Now what have I done?"

"You're an accountant. You have to know the price, so give me a range!"

"Nope. Promise me you won't consider the cost. I'll worry about that." His grin faded, and he took her arm and started to walk again. "Leah and I carried large insurance policies. I've inherited a sizable sum," he said bitterly. His voice returned to normal as he added, "I'm a frugal accountant. You've seen how I live. I have savings that—to put it modestly—are sufficient to enable me to afford the picture you select. Before long I'm going to use some of those funds to go into business for myself."

"I remember. You told me that before."

"This afternoon I want to show you sites I've picked out that might be good for my office."

He held open the door to a gallery and she entered, glancing briefly at him as she brushed past, her thoughts on the fact that he was putting down roots as quickly as possible.

With dramatic effect, the place had white walls and strategic lighting to emphasize the artwork. Indian pottery contrasted artistically with the oil paintings and Navajo rugs on display. As Savannah moved around the room, she was shocked to see the prices on the paintings. Amazed, she glanced at Mike.

He stood with his back to her, his hands in the pockets of his jeans, while he studied a collage that resembled a desert scene. She reassessed her thinking about his situation, realizing that if he could casually walk in and buy any painting in this gallery without giving a thought to the price, he was an extremely wealthy man. That fact made her view him in a slightly different light, and she was puzzled by her own feelings, because a quiet discomfort nagged at her over her discovery. When he glanced over his shoulder at her, she returned her attention to the paintings.

The owner of the gallery waited on them. They had a polite, friendly conversation, but Savannah didn't see anything she particularly liked or thought Mike would like.

When they were outside she turned to him. "This is crazy! You pick out what you like."

He shook his head. "Absolutely not. They all look the same to me. You show me what to get."

"Okay, but it seems a ridiculous way to spend a lot of money."

"Humor me," he whispered in her ear, tickling her.

"Mike!"

Chuckling, he held open the door of another gallery. After one look at the price below the first picture, Savannah drew a sharp breath and turned to whisper to Mike. "This place is definitely too expensive!"

"You have a mighty short memory. I told you to ignore the prices," Mike said quietly.

She stared at the neat figure of twelve thousand three hundred dollars and suddenly felt cold. Mike wasn't quite the man she had thought he was all along, and she had a sinking feeling that he might not be the settled family man she had wanted him to be.

"Do you like that one?" he asked.

"What? Oh, maybe." She saw a question in his gaze and moved away from him.

In less than five minutes she spotted a painting she felt she could look at endlessly. She motioned to him to join her. "I like this one, Mike. But it's not an oil. It's a watercolor. And it's entirely too expensive!" she added as she looked again at a price higher than any she had seen.

They gazed at the picture of a landscape with sweeping clouds above a hillside, the colors varied from delicate blues to deep greens.

"That's a good selection," a quiet male voice said behind them, and they turned to meet the art consultant. "It's a John Constable landscape." He extended his hand. "I'm Henry Fenworth."

Mike introduced Savannah and himself, then turned back to the painting, staring at it a moment before asking Savannah, "You like that the best?"

"Yes, but perhaps we should look around. We just started shopping."

Mike agreed, and they moved on after Henry Fenworth had told them he would answer any questions they might have.

They roamed through the gallery, then went to two more. Later, as Savannah looked back on the day, she realized how swiftly and by what small incidents her total outlook had changed. As she moved around a gallery, looking at Indian art, Mike drifted away from her to the other side of the room. Savannah heard a bell tinkle over the door when another customer entered, but she didn't look around. When she paused in front of a painting of an Indian on horseback in a snowstorm, she heard a lilting voice say, "Mike. Hello!"

Nine

"Hi, Kathy," Mike answered easily. Savannah glanced around to see Mike turn toward a brunette who had stopped a few feet from him. Her hair was stylishly cut, short and swept high on the sides. Her profile was to Savannah, who noticed how lovely, tall, and slender the woman was.

"I didn't know you liked art," the woman said.

"Sure," he answered, and glanced toward Savannah, who returned her attention to the painting on the wall.

"The picnic was fun. In spite of Madge's efforts. I do hope you'll forgive her."

Savannah didn't want to eavesdrop, so she moved along to the next painting, but she felt numb with shock. There was no mistaking the warmth in the brunette's voice. And for the first time Savannah realized that if Mike wanted to establish himself in Santa Fe and start his own business, he would need to make local contacts. His interests were changing swiftly and totally from Minnesota and all he had known, including her.

"Savannah."

She turned to see Mike motioning her to join him. The brunette turned also, and Savannah saw her eyebrows arch in surprise.

"Come meet Kathy Vernon. Kathy, this is Savannah Carson."

They exchanged greetings. Then Kathy smiled at Mike and said, "Well, I'll leave you two to your shopping. I'll see you Wednesday night, Mike."

"Sure, Kathy."

"It was nice to meet you," Savannah said, wondering what Mike would be doing on Wednesday—and Monday and Tuesday and all the other nights in his life when she wasn't around.

As soon as they were alone Mike explained, "She's a friend someone's wife introduced me to. I'm the new widower in town."

"And in demand," she said quietly, looking away. Then she changed the subject. "I like the Constable watercolor the best, but it costs a fortune."

"Let's go back and look at it," he said cheerfully, as if totally unaware of her stormy emotions. Outside the midday sun beat down, making Savannah feel queasy and light-headed.

When she ran her hand across her brow, Mike noticed, and he frowned. "Do you feel all right?"

"I'm warm," she admitted.

"Sit down in the shade of a tree," Mike ordered. He steered her to a bench on a grassy patch in the center of the Plaza. Sidewalks laced the square of cottonwoods and benches, and a cool breeze gave her relief.

"I'll be right back," he said.

She leaned back, watching him stride away. Her brief dizziness passed, and in a short time Mike returned. He had an iced drink in each hand, and he handed her one as he sat down beside her.

"The painting has been purchased and will be delivered. How do you feel?"

"Much better. Thanks for the drink."

"I thought you might like it. See the Palace of the Governors over there?"

While she looked at the rambling adobe building Mike said, "It's where the Spanish, Indian, Mexican, and American territorial governors lived. In the late 1800s the territorial Governor, Lew Wallace, lived there when he wrote *Ben Hur*. The Indians have the right to sell their wares under the portico."

She listened while Mike talked, keeping her mind on his account of Santa Fe history, refusing to think about the fragility of their relationship.

Finally he asked, "Want to go home?"

"No, I'm fine now."

He looked at her searchingly, and she smiled, feeling as if she were standing on a high wire and that the slightest wrong move would send her tumbling.

"Come on. We'll look at the cathedral. It was built in 1869 by Archbishop Jean Baptiste Lamy. I read that he missed the Romanesque style of architecture in his homeland, France, so he finally built his own church here."

Mike's continual informative talk was interesting, but Savannah found it increasingly difficult to keep her attention on Santa Fe instead of on Mike. As they walked through the Museum of Fine Arts, she studied Mike while he talked about Navajo sand paintings. She wanted to feel his arms around her. In a little over twenty-four hours she would be on her way back to Duluth, separated from him again. The hunger she felt for his kisses was as tangible to her as the paintings on the walls.

Mike studied the picture in front of him. Its effect had been achieved through the Navajo tradition of using crushed rock, minerals, and sand on masonite. As he talked about the history of the craft, he glanced at Savannah.

She was looking at him intently. Her lips were slightly parted, her cheeks pink, her eyes half-closed, with a sensual, sleepy expression, and he forgot every word he had said or intended to say. Suddenly he wanted her, and he saw desire clearly written in her expression. He sucked in his breath, aware of what her thoughts must be, the realization inflaming him. He slipped his arm around her waist, moving closer to whisper. "Want to go home? Brian's gone for the day."

She nodded, and together they left. As they entered the cool house, Mike locked the door behind them and turned to take Savannah in his arms.

"What you do to me . . ." he said, then leaned forward to place his lips over hers.

Consumed by roaring flames of passion, she held him tightly, wanting to hold him forever.

That night Brian joined them for dinner at the Pink Adobe, on Old Santa Fe Trail. They were led to an alcove and given menus that listed Santa Fe specialties. Hoping the green chiles wouldn't be too spicy, Savannah ordered chicken enchiladas. Along with the dinners, Mike ordered *sopaipillas*, puffy pastries served with honey, and *posole*, a dish of hominy cooked with pork and chile.

Dinner was delicious, and Mike seemed happy about how well she got along with Brian. It was easy to get along with him—he had inherited his father's charm.

At one point during the evening Mike said, "You saw my hedge of lilacs. They grow all over Santa Fe, and everyone tells me what a sight they are in April."

"They say the whole town smells like lilacs," Brian added.

"Lilacs in April," Savannah said, looking at Mike

and thinking she would like a huge bouquet of lilacs
when their baby was born. Mike raised his head and
met her gaze. His brows arched and he tilted his
head to one side.

"Do you like lilacs?" he asked.

"Very much. I want a bouquet of them," she said,
and saw the puzzlement in Mike's eyes. She ached
to reach across the table and take his hand and tell
him exactly when she wanted the bouquet and why.

"You can have plenty from our yard," Brian said,
oblivious of undercurrents. "I saw a good show last
night," he continued, and there was no more talk of
lilacs.

On Sunday morning Savannah helped Brian with
a paper he was writing for a correspondence course
on Byron and Keats. They worked in the rustic
kitchen, which already held some of Savannah's clutter. Her new gifts, her sweater, and a magazine she
was reading were scattered around.

At one point she looked up to find Brian studying
her. He had his head propped against his hand as
he lounged in a kitchen chair, his elbow on the table
and his foot on the seat of another chair.

"You're good for Dad. I'm glad you two met," he
said frankly.

"Thank you," she said, sincerely pleased.

"He's had a tough time. I hated to be gone through
the trial, but we talked it over and I had the feeling I
would be of more help by being out of the country
than by staying with him."

"I think you're right, because they could have gotten at him through you."

"I'm glad it's over." He continued to stare at her.

"What's on your mind?"

He shrugged. "You look young. I'm impressed with

my father. I sort of think of him as . . . just Dad, not a guy who dates women."

She laughed. "I'm thirty-six, Brian."

"You are?" His genuine shock pleased her, and she nodded.

"I'm almost finished reading," she said, bending over his paper once again.

"I think he's worked you long enough," Mike said from the doorway. As he came into the room, Savannah wondered how long he had been watching them and what he had heard. Her heart beat more quickly as she scooted her chair over to make room for him beside her.

"I only have a little more to read, and I want to finish. This is interesting."

"Keats?" Mike said. "Never heard of him."

"He's a poet, Dad."

"You're reading poetry?"

"It's for my class."

"Shh." Savannah gave them a mock frown and returned to the paper. When she finished she gave it to Brian. He thanked her and held out his right hand.

"I have to go now, Savannah, and I won't be back until late tonight. It was good to meet you."

"Thank you, Brian," she said, giving his hand a firm shake. He winked, reminding her more strongly of Mike. Brian was attractive, likable, and she felt as if they were friends and had started off on the right foot with each other. And briefly she wondered what he would think if he knew he would soon have a half-brother or -sister.

To her dismay the day passed far too swiftly. When Sunday night came and it was time for her flight home, Mike took her to the airport, kissed her good-bye, and gave her a ticket to come back the next weekend.

She sat on the plane, looking down at the lights of Santa Fe, while she turned the ticket over in her hand and thought about the weekend. Never once had Mike mentioned a lasting commitment. Yet she knew he loved her. And he wanted her back next week. She bit her lip as she thought about him. His wealth, his new life and friends, his obvious love of Santa Fe, the brunette, Kathy. Mike might be making a new niche for himself and not need or want her after a few more months.

It would be just a matter of time before he ended the relationship, she told herself. A small knot of fear and anguish began to torment her as she wondered if she had been fooling herself all along.

Three days after she had arrived home, Savannah stretched out on her bed to rest after coming home from school. All she could think about was that it was Wednesday and Kathy Vernon would see Mike that night. The doorbell rang, interrupting her thoughts, and Savannah greeted a delivery man with a package. She signed for the delivery and stared at the large box as he carried it inside. As soon as the man was gone, she bent over the package, to see the name of a Santa Fe art gallery in the corner. Shock held her immobile for a moment. Then she got a kitchen knife and swiftly opened the package. Inside was the Constable watercolor she had selected for Mike.

Tears threatened to spill from her eyes as she picked up the card Mike must have written while she sat on the bench in the shade of the tree. "With love and thanks for taking me in when I needed someone . . . Mike."

She pressed the card to her heart and stared at the picture through shimmering tears. "Mike," she whispered. She loved the painting, but she wanted something more than a lovely, expensive watercolor—she wanted Mike's love, with a desperate need that seemed to grow daily.

"I love you," she whispered to the empty room. She tried to call him, but it wasn't until half-past five that he answered.

She lay back in bed, trying to picture him in his tight jeans and shirt. "You shouldn't have done it," she said quietly, and closed her eyes as she listened to his voice.

"I wanted you to have it and I couldn't pick something out."

Her throat tightened and she clutched the phone, unable to talk.

"Savannah?"

"Mike, it's too much!"

"Hey, you're crying!"

"I love you."

"Well, Lordy, don't cry! I thought it would make you happy, not sad."

"It does! You're sweet," she said, and fought for control. "I've never had a gift like that before."

"You deserve it. What I'd like to give you . . ." His voice dropped as he paused, and a husky note came into his tone that strummed over her nerves and changed her emotions. "I'd like to start at your ankles, Savannah, and kiss you slowly . . ." His voice thickened and slowed, and she gripped the phone, suddenly feeling on fire. "Where are you now?" he asked.

"On my bed."

He groaned. "Savannah . . . I can't wait until Friday."

"You're going to see Kathy tonight." The words were out before she could stop them. There was a moment of silence; then she broke into it.

"Mike, I'm sorry. It's none—"

"Honey, Kathy is a friend of a friend's wife and I'm going to a company dinner party tonight, and I can't remember what color hair Kathy has or what color eyes, or if she's fat or skinny—"

"Mike, stop!" she said, laughing and crying at the same time and hating her sudden inability to control her emotions.

"That's better," he said. He sounded sincere, making her thankful that he'd only heard her laughter. "I have to go to a boring company dinner party, but I only want to be with you. By the way, you made a hit with Brian."

"He's great! I'm glad. I liked him too."

"I think if he had half a chance, he'd ask you out himself."

"Don't be ridiculous! I'm old enough to be his mother."

"I don't think he sees you that way. I'm glad you two got along."

"He's like you, absolutely charming."

"Savannah, don't say things like that when we're hundreds of miles apart!"

She laughed, holding the phone tightly and closing her eyes. "If you only knew, Mike," she said in a throaty whisper. "I'm remembering how you look when we're in bed, how your eyes darken, how your body—"

"Savannah! I can't take that!" he said roughly, and suddenly all teasing was gone from his voice.

"I love you," she whispered, holding the phone tightly. "I have to go, Mike. Enjoy your party." She hung up without waiting to hear his reply.

Savannah spent the next two weekends with Mike, and he said no more about a commitment than he had during her previous visits. In the middle of the third week in September he called her from St. Paul to tell her his uncle Grant had died suddenly.

"Mike, I can get a plane to St. Paul and be there tonight."

"You don't need to," he answered. "You have to teach, and I'm all right. We're having a simple service Friday and I'll fly home Saturday. This cancels our time together on the weekend."

"I'll be glad to come to St. Paul. I hate it when you're alone."

"I'm fine. Uncle Grant had a good, long life. Honey, don't worry about me. And don't leave. I know how busy you must be."

They talked long and often over the next few days, while he was in St. Paul and then after he had returned to Santa Fe. Though Savannah missed him terribly, they planned to see each other as soon as possible. But other things kept interfering with their plans.

During the last week in September Mike had to fly back to St. Paul to take care of legal matters. Then he was detained on the weekend. The next weekend, October fourth, she was busy as class sponsor for the Homecoming festivities. And the next weekend was the annual Blair reunion. The kernels of worry that had plagued Savannah in early fall grew into monumental fears. To add to her misery, she hadn't been feeling well. Teaching was a drain, and Duluth had an early cold spell, which made her realize time was passing swiftly.

She finally faced the fact that Mike had never intended to make a permanent commitment. The first time she voiced what she felt was to Ginny. Her sister had stopped by her house after school one day. As Ginny sat drinking coffee at the kitchen table while Savannah placed a frozen dinner in the oven, Ginny's brow furrowed in a frown.

"Savannah, you have to tell Mike."

"No!" She ran her hand through her hair, closed the oven door, and walked over to the table. She pulled out the chair quickly and sat down, closing her eyes.

"Are you all right?" Ginny asked.

"Yes. I think so."

"You look terrible."

"I feel light-headed."

"Have you seen Dr. Borden?"

"I have an appointment on Friday the twenty-fourth."

"Are you going to Santa Fe this weekend?"

"No. Mike's going to fly to Houston to visit a friend and go to a football game—something he says he planned before he met me."

"By the time you next see him you won't be able to keep your pregnancy from him."

"Then I won't go to see him."

Ginny stared at her sister for a long moment. Then her tone of voice changed. "See Dr. Borden," she said gently. "I'm glad you told everyone, but you have two brothers who would like to throttle the man in your life!"

"I know, but they promised me they would behave. They're so good to me. Ginny, I don't know what's happening to me. I feel weepy over the slightest thing, and then I feel jubilant. When I think about my baby I'm so happy I could dance on the roof. I want to stop strangers in the grocery store and tell them I'm pregnant. Wait, let me show you what I have!"

She left and came back with a dress. "Look at this! Isn't it great?"

"It looks like a flowered tent."

"I know. And I can't wait to wear it."

"Wait until you're knee-deep in diapers," Ginny said dryly.

"I'll love it."

"I think you mean it." Ginny looked at her watch. "I have to run. I wish you'd tell him. Any man who would spend what he did on that picture for you should be willing to marry you and give his child a father and a name."

"We'll see."

"I know what that means. It means you'll do it your way, come hell or high water. You see the doctor or I'll tell Mom on you!"

Savannah laughed and nodded as she said goodbye to her sister. After Ginny had gone she placed her hand on her stomach. "Mike," she whispered, and rubbed her abdomen. She hadn't heard from Mike in three days—a first. She shrugged and went to her room to lie down.

The next week, on Thursday, the twenty-third of October, at two o'clock, Savannah was in the middle of her planning period at school. She was sitting at her desk, talking to a fifteen-year-old student about whether the girl should marry a man nine years her senior. Savannah was filing papers while she talked, when suddenly she felt a tight cramp in her stomach.

"Oh!" She bent over slightly, holding her waist.

"Mrs. Carson, are you all right?" Ivy asked.

"Yes," Savannah said automatically, but she wasn't. She hurt badly. She drew a sharp breath and blinked, clutching the desk.

"Are you sure you're all right?"

"I will be," she answered, but her voice was so weak, it seemed to be coming from a long distance.

Fear such as she had never known before enveloped her, as though cold claws were digging into her heart.

Please, God, let me be all right, she prayed.

"Mrs. Carson?"

"I'm okay, Ivy. I just need to put my head down for a moment." She laid her head on the desk, but the room spun and another cramp made her gasp from the pain.

"Mrs. Carson, I'll go get Miss White."

"I'm all right," Savannah said, but she could barely hear her own voice. Suddenly she had a tearing pain in her stomach and she cried out, clutching at her side. The room spun and she felt alternately hot and cold and boneless.

"Ivy . . ."

"Mrs. Carson, what—"

The girl rushed to Savannah's side, and then blackness closed in as Savannah lost consciousness.

Ten

Savannah came to as they were lifting her onto a stretcher. Faces floated above her, and she tried to speak.

"It's okay, Savannah," she heard someone say, and she looked up at the calm face of Nadine White, the school nurse.

"Mike," she whispered; then a swirling blackness enveloped her again.

When she stirred once more and opened her eyes, she was confused, and could hear the wailing of a siren.

Fear stabbed her as she became aware of pain, and she placed her hands on her stomach. "No!" she tried to cry out. "Our baby—"

"Shh, Savannah. We're on the way to St. Mary's Hospital."

"Dr. Borden . . ." she whispered, barely able to form the words. She felt as if she were slipping into a black pool that was pulling her down. "No . . . please . . ."

The next time she opened her eyes she heard her name.

"Savannah."

She tried to think, but it took too much effort. She knew someone was talking to her. A face blurred in front of her, then came into focus, and she could have sobbed with relief as she recognized the familiar brown eyes and freckled face of Dr. Borden.

"My baby!" she said with a suffocating sense of desperation.

"Quiet," he said gently, pressing her shoulder. "You're going to be all right."

She wanted to cry out that she wasn't worried about herself. It was Mike's baby whom she wanted protected. "Our baby . . . please don't let—"

"Savannah, you and the baby will be all right," he said calmly, but she wasn't convinced. She clutched at his wrist. "Our baby . . . Mike . . . Mike!"

She slipped from consciousness and drifted into blackness again. When she stirred the next time, she was in a hospital room. She tried to remember what had happened and where she was, while she studied the beige walls and the blank television located high on a shelf beyond the foot of her bed. When her memory returned, she cried out.

"Savannah, are you all right?" came a concerned, familiar voice.

She turned to see her mother scoot closer to the bed and reach out to take her hand.

"Mom?" Instantly she remembered. "My baby—"

"You're all right and your baby is all right," her mother said quietly. "Dr. Borden will be back to explain everything to you, but you're going to be okay, and if you're careful the baby will be okay."

Savannah could barely comprehend what her mother had said. The words echoed in her mind. She wanted Mike's strong arms around her. She wanted someone to say their baby was fine. ". . . *if you're careful the baby will be okay . . . if you're careful . . .*" The words were a haunting refrain, and she tried to ask her mother what she had meant, but her voice wouldn't come. She closed her eyes and took a deep breath, concentrating on asking the questions that plagued her, but instead she drifted to sleep.

"Ah, how's my patient?" Dr. Borden asked.

Savannah had no idea how much time had passed, when she opened her eyes to see Dr. Borden smiling at her and holding her wrist to take her pulse. "Feel better?"

"What about the baby?"

He waited a moment to check her pulse, then lowered her arm to the bed and looked into her eyes.

"You're anemic, overworked, and you're under an emotional strain. On top of that you're facing recurrent uterine bleeding." He leaned closer and rubbed her arm, stirring her to alertness.

"Do you want a baby?"

"You know how much—"

"Okay, young lady. No teaching."

"I have—" She stopped abruptly as she stared into his implacable face.

He shook his head. "If you want to give birth to your baby at the proper time, you need bed rest. That means no teaching, no housework, no sex. You stay in bed and watch soaps until next spring."

Savannah stared at him as the words sank into her mind. No teaching—no salary. No housework . . . staying in bed.

She gritted her teeth and rubbed her stomach. She had savings, and if it took her last nickel, she would do exactly what Dr. Borden instructed. "I'll do it," she said.

"All the time. You're not accustomed to lounging

around and letting others wait on you, but anytime you think about working or getting up, remember what the outcome might be."

"I understand," she answered solemnly, knowing that Dr. Borden had a good idea of how badly she wanted her baby.

"That's my girl. You do like your old doctor says, and we'll deliver this baby, come spring."

"Yes, sir."

"And you, Mrs. Blair, see to it that your daughter does just what she should."

"We will. There's an army of us to keep watch."

"I know. All of us want you to have this baby, Savannah," he said gently. She tried to smile at him, but a knot burned in her throat.

Dr. Borden left, and her mother scooted closer again. "Can I bring you anything?"

"No, thanks. Thanks for coming, Mom."

"You know I would always come, always do anything to help. Savannah, can I call Mike?"

Savannah shook her head. "No. Please. All of you promised . . ." she whispered, feeling exhaustion tug at her.

"We'll keep our promises until you say differently, but I think you should let him know."

"No, Mom. I know what I'm doing." She turned her head and drifted off to sleep. When she opened her eyes again, the room was dusky and dim. A light from the hall spilled a yellow wedge through the partially opened door, and Savannah saw the empty chair where her mother had been and the darkened window, and guessed it was late at night.

"Mike," she whispered, finally giving vent to the longings and hurt that had swamped her like quicksand since her first moments of pain and fear. She ached for him. Again she rubbed her hands over her stomach as if to reassure herself the baby was safe.

She squeezed her eyes tightly shut, her lips moving in a silent prayer that her baby would live and be normal.

Despair, longing, and fear were like invisible demons dancing in the shadows of the room. She wanted Mike's strength and comfort. She was terrified for the baby. And she felt a forlorn sense of isolation. If only she wouldn't lose her baby, she thought, she could survive all else. . . .

"Mike," she whispered again, knotting the sheet in her hands and fighting the threatening tears. She took deep breaths and tried to will her thoughts elsewhere, frightened that if she sobbed it might jeopardize the baby's welfare. She tried to think of something else, shifting her thoughts to school and what she would have to do to help the teacher who would take her place.

The next day her family came, a few at a time. They stayed so briefly, Savannah was sure Dr. Borden had suggested that they keep their visits short. They brought presents—magazines and books and flowers.

Late in the afternoon she heard a rap on the door, and opened her eyes to see three faces in the doorway. "Come in," she said, smiling.

Three of her students, Tina, Stephanie, and Ivy, walked into the room. They looked curious and uncertain as Stephanie timidly held out a pot of white mums. "This is from your third-hour class. We hope you'll be back soon."

"What lovely flowers! Thank you so much. And please let everyone know how much I like them." Savannah couldn't tell them yet that she wouldn't be back, because the principal had to be the first to know. "This is my mother, Mrs. Blair. Mom, I want you to meet Ivy Ridgeview, Stephanie Miller, and Tina Wharton."

They chatted about school, and after a few minutes the girls said good-bye. No sooner had they gone than the principal appeared. Savannah's mother talked with him for a moment, then went alone into the hall. While her mother was gone, Savannah told Dr. James that she wouldn't be able to return to teaching.

As soon as he was gone, her mother came back into the room. "Did you tell him?"

Savannah was staring at the window, seeing only the blue sky outside. "Yes." She turned her head. "I'm sorry to be leaving, but it wasn't as hard as I thought it would be."

"I knew you'd manage. The new teacher will do just fine—the same way you did when you started."

"I don't know what I would do without my family."

Her mother centered the pot of mums, which now sat on the shelf beside the television. "I have to go now, Savannah. Ginny will be up tonight. Is there anything you want her to bring you?"

"No, thanks."

"See you later."

Savannah felt exhausted and closed her eyes, thinking how swiftly her life had changed and how many changes lay ahead. And she finally faced the concern she had put out of her mind since she had regained consciousness. She knew she would have to break off contact with Mike. The pain she felt this time was higher, because it was around her heart, but it was just as tangible. Yet she had no other choice. If Mike knew about the baby, he would insist on a marriage he didn't really want, and she couldn't have stood that. The only way to keep him from knowing was to stop seeing him.

She wiped her eyes, and gritted her teeth so fiercely, her jaw ached. Picking up the phone, she placed the call to New Mexico.

Mike's voice was almost her undoing. She clutched the phone and wasn't able to speak at first.

"Hello? Hello?" he repeated impatiently.

For an instant she was tempted to hang up and try to make the call later, but later it might only be worse. "Mike," she said, his name only a whisper.

"Savannah?"

"Yes."

"I tried to call you for hours last night."

"Sorry, Mike, I was busy."

"I have seats for the races next Saturday, and I mailed you a plane ticket. The extracurricular activities are over at school, aren't they?"

"Yes, but I can't come."

There was a pause. "I miss you, Savannah. I'd like you to come see me."

"Mike, I can't come to Santa Fe. . . ." Quickly she moved the phone away from her mouth, twisting the receiver so she could hear him, as she fought to hold back a sob. She squeezed her eyes closed while she listened to the silence, imagining his shock.

"You're sure you can't come next weekend?" he asked in the solemn, angry voice she had heard him use so often during the trial.

She bit her lip and took a deep breath. "I'm sorry, but no. And not after next weekend either. Things have changed, Mike. I have my life here, and you have yours there." She placed the phone on the bed, pressing it against the mattress while she cried. She couldn't hear what he was saying, but she didn't want him to hear her cry.

She took another breath and put the receiver against her ear.

". . . say it plainly?" he asked harshly, and she had to guess at what he'd said.

"I just have my life, Mike. Can we leave it at that? We've known from the first . . ."

"Yeah," he said gruffly. "Is there another man?"

"Mike, I want to say good-bye. I have to go. I . . . That's just all I can say."

"Savannah, why—" He broke off abruptly. "Can you come down in two weeks?"

"No. Mike, please . . . just say good-bye. That's the way we planned it from the first."

Her heart beat wildly as the silence went on and on, and she could imagine the angry scowl he probably had on his face. If only . . . if only he had loved her deeply enough . . .

"Good-bye, Savannah," he said sharply. The phone clicked in her ear and it was over.

She wanted to sob hysterically, but she forced herself to think about school, and not about Mike, because she was afraid of the effect her depression might have on the baby. *I'll cry in April,* she told herself, knowing that was absurd, but needing to do anything she could to try to keep from yielding to the flood of tears that threatened.

She picked up a pair of blue booties that her mother had brought and smoothed them in her hand, and her spirits lifted. She kept the baby gifts her family had brought close to the bed, where she could look at them and think only positive thoughts about the baby.

"Jeff," she said aloud.

"Hi."

She looked up to see Ginny at the door. Ginny looked around. "Who's Jeff?"

Savannah wiped her eyes and smiled, patting her stomach. "Jefferson Michael Blair. How do you like the name I've selected?"

"It's great, and when she's born are we going to call her Jeffersona?"

"Very funny," Savannah said, aware Ginny would notice immediately that she had been crying.

"No kidding. What will you do if it's a girl?"

"Then she'll be Michelle Margaret Blair."

"Ah, Margaret, named after Mom. Are you dropping Carson?"

"Yes. My baby won't have Tyler's name," Savannah said firmly. "I'll go back to Savannah Blair."

"How're you feeling?"

"Exhausted."

"I brought you a present."

"Another one! Ginny, all of you need to stop."

"We're doing it because we want to. And this is something little that Jill helped pick out."

Savannah unwrapped the blue paper from around a square box and pulled out a stuffed yellow bunny. She wound it up and listened to it play a familiar tune about Peter Cottontail. She smiled as she smoothed the rabbit's whiskers. "Thank you, and tell Jill I like her selection."

"I will. I saw Dr. Borden, and he said you can go home tomorrow. I'll come get you as soon as you're ready."

"Good," Savannah said, setting the rabbit on the bed beside her hip. "I wanted to get the nursery ready for the baby, but now I can't."

"You know you have a dozen people who are willing and able, and experienced at getting nurseries ready."

"That's true."

There was a long moment of silence. "You talked to Mike today, didn't you?"

Savannah nodded. She picked up the rabbit and tried to imagine her baby holding it.

"I don't suppose you had a change of heart and told him."

"No," Savannah answered, refusing to tell Ginny that she had ended her relationship with Mike. She knew what a storm it would stir up in her family, and she wasn't about to tell any of them yet.

"I didn't come up here to worry you," Ginny said, her concern evident in her voice and in her expression, as her brow creased in a frown. "What colors would you like in the nursery? As if I needed to ask—blue, I'm sure."

"You're right. How'd you guess! Blue like his daddy's ey—" She broke off abruptly, feeling stricken.

"Oh, Savannah," Ginny said sadly. "Tell him!"

Savannah took a deep breath, raised her chin, and said, "I can't do it. I'm not going to cry over him until next spring, Ginny. It might upset the baby."

Ginny's eyes became round. "That's the craziest thing I've—Okay. Next spring the tears come with the tulips. What color besides blue?"

Savannah focused her thoughts on the nursery and the baby, and soon her breathing returned to normal and the tension went out of her shoulders. "I guess white."

"Traditional. Okay."

They talked about decorations and Ginny's children, until Ginny said she had to pick up Ted junior from football practice.

"See you tomorrow. We have a schedule all worked out. We'll take turns staying with you and doing all your errands and chores. And someday you'll have to pay us back—each and every one! We'll keep track of the hours."

Savannah was torn between laughter and tears, because she knew none of them would want to be paid back. "You are all so good to me."

"Wait until you have to baby-sit on Saturday nights," Ginny said airily. "See you later."

At noon the next day Ginny was back at the hospital with Jill, and she was full of cheer and talk as a nurse helped Savannah into the car.

Home looked wonderful to Savannah, and she sank down on the sofa while Ginny puttered around the room arranging bouquets of flowers, turning on the television, and talking constantly.

Savannah had discovered that planning the nursery kept her cheerful and full of anticipation, and she alternately focused her attention on that or on trying to make a list of everything a new teacher might want to know about her classes and curricula.

Mike was a closed subject. No one in the family mentioned him, and she immediately turned her thoughts to the baby or to school every time he came to mind. Which was about every ten minutes. At eight o'clock that night she was congratulating herself on how well she had gotten through the day, when the phone rang. Her mother was spending the night, and she picked up the phone and handed it to Savannah.

As soon as Savannah heard Mike's deep voice she said, "Hi, Mike." Immediately her mother gathered up her sewing and left the room.

"Savannah, I'd like to talk," he said in as gruff a voice as he had used before.

The familiar ache started inside her, but she took a deep breath and tried to answer in a cheerful tone. "All right, Mike, but there's really not much to talk about."

"You know I can't risk coming back to Duluth."

"I don't expect you to, and there's no reason for you to take a risk."

"Well, hell. Yes there is, if you won't come to Santa Fe."

"I can't come."

"You mean you won't come," he said in a tone that cut her like a knife.

"I guess if you want to put it that way. There's no point in your coming here, and I'm not coming to New Mexico. There are other things in my life right now."

"Dammit, can't we talk about it? Isn't this sort of abrupt?"

"Not really."

There was a long, long pause; then suddenly he snapped, "Sorry, I bothered you, Savannah!"

The phone clicked, and she replaced the receiver. Immediately she picked up the yellow bunny, wound it up, and stroked it while it played its tune.

That was the last she heard from Mike. The days passed, and gradually her strength returned. It was tempting to get out of bed, but she intended to do exactly as Dr. Borden had ordered. Almost two weeks after she had been released from the hospital, she answered the phone and heard a familiar deep voice.

"Mike?" she asked, forgetting to keep her tone subdued.

"No, Savannah, it's Brian."

"Brian? Are you in Duluth?"

"Yeah, for the weekend. Can I come over and see you? I told Dad I'd call."

Stunned, she sat up in bed. Seeing Brian wasn't something she had planned on, and if he came over, he would inform Mike exactly how she was. And she couldn't tell Brian she was pregnant! Her mind raced.

"It's nice that you're here."

"Yeah. Can I come by in an hour?"

She ran her fingers distractedly through her hair. "Brian, I'm sorry, but you can't."

"Savannah, Dad asked me to talk to you." He was as solemn as Mike sometimes had sounded. "You know his life is in danger if he comes to Duluth."

"I know." Her mind was searching for something to tell Brian, and the silence became too long. "I'm sorry."

"Savannah, if I can't talk to you, he'll come up here."

"He doesn't need to. You can't come over because . . . because . . . I have the mumps."

"*Mumps?*" He sounded incredulous, and she could hardly blame him.

"Yes. Have you had the shot for it?"

"No. I don't know," he said, sounding perplexed. "I don't remember. How'd you get the mumps?"

"From teaching school, I guess."

"Are you very sick?"

"Yes. I'm sorry I can't see you, but I can't have visitors."

"I'm sorry too."

"Tell your father I said hello, and tell him I would like to have talked with you, but there really isn't much point, Brian. I've already talked to your dad."

There was another pause, and finally he said, "Well, Savannah, Dad's . . . Well, he gave me plane tickets to give you. He's going to call you tonight, and he wants you to come to Santa Fe some weekend soon."

"I can't, Brian, and I'll tell him that when I talk to him. Take the tickets back with you. I'll make it clear to him. I have to go now. It hurts to talk."

"Oh! Sorry. Sorry you're sick. Good-bye, Savannah," he said, sounding just like his father.

She hung up the phone, and leaned her head back against the sofa.

"Trouble?" Brit asked, running her hand through curls that were as blond as Savannah's hair.

"It was Mike's son, Brian. He wanted to come see me, and I told him I have mumps."

"Mumps!" Brit stared at Savannah with so much shock in her wide eyes that Savannah had to laugh.

"It was all I could think of to keep him away. I can't see him like this." She patted her waist, which was beginning to thicken. Then she quickly changed the subject, not wanting to dwell on thoughts of Mike. "I hate to just sit here and watch you clean."

"I'll let you make it up to me after the baby comes. You can baby-sit the kids more often."

"I'd love to."

"Oh, I was kidding!"

"There won't be anything wrong with me after I have my baby, and I won't be going out on Saturday nights. You know how I love to have your children over."

Brit paused to stare at her sister. "Mumps, babies, and single parenting. You ought to tell him, Savannah. He obviously loves you a little. I'd settle for that."

"I've been through a marriage where love died on the vine. No, thanks. And I don't think you would settle for it either."

Brit tilted her head as she considered it, and finally she shrugged. "I guess I might not if Logan had said from the very first time we met that he wasn't going to marry. I'll keep my nose out of your business."

"Don't be silly!"

"I'm going to get the laundry."

"Bring it in here. I can fold a little at a time without getting up."

"No way!"

Savannah smiled, thinking how her family was pampering her and how she would be able to repay all of them later. Then her thoughts returned to Brian. How good his voice had sounded! It wasn't Brian the voice conjured up, but the image of Mike. Mike. She wondered if it would ever stop hurting. She knew she would have to tell Mike about his child at some point. When and how would she ever do it?

She shoved that question aside. It was too worri-some to contemplate at the moment. She watched puppets cavorting on television, but her mind was on Mike and the tickets he had sent. He must miss her, to have sent Brian to Duluth with plane tickets for her.

How she wished things were different! He had said he loved her. Yet all he wanted was for her to come for weekend visits. That wasn't enough. Not any longer.

Half an hour later Brian sank down on the bed in the room of one of his childhood friends. He was alone at Jack's, and he used his father's phone credit card to place a call.

After two rings Mike answered.

"Dad, I called Savannah."

"Are you going to see her?"

"No. That's why I called. She said there wasn't any reason to give her the tickets—she won't be coming to Santa Fe."

"Did she say anything else? I wanted you to go by and see her."

"I couldn't. She has the mumps." Brian stretched out on the bed, propping up his stockinged feet.

"Mumps?"

"That's what she said." Brian wondered about his dad and Savannah. Savannah was gorgeous, and Brian liked her. And he knew his father was deeply in love with her. He could understand why, and he was sorry it wasn't working out, but she had sounded adamant and uninterested on the phone. And she hadn't sounded as if she had the mumps.

"Thanks for calling her, Brian. How's Jack?"

"He's fine. I'm at his house now."

"Good. Tell his family hello for me. I'd like to be there too." Brian heard the rough note in his father's voice and hated the fact that his Dad was going through another upheaval in his life. "Dad, there are a lot of good-looking women in Santa Fe. And there are a lot who are dying to date you."

"Yeah, but it's not the same. I'll meet you at the airport tomorrow. Be careful while you're there."

"I'm not going anywhere until Jack takes me to the plane."

"Okay. See you," Mike said, and hung up the phone. Brian replaced the receiver and stared thoughtfully into space.

A week later Mike sat in his kitchen, his dinner on the table in front of him, barely touched. Mumps, he thought. Savannah had the mumps. That was the flimsiest, sorriest excuse he had ever heard in his life! But why? Why had she put Brian off with such a gosh-awful excuse? He knew to his toes that Savannah Blair Carson did not have the mumps.

He remembered that sickening, frightful moment when the gunshot had shattered the window of his car, but he had to go back to Duluth and see Savannah. Something was terribly wrong.

Since her first refusal to come to Santa Fe, Mike had figured there was a new man in Savannah's life. And, too late, he'd seen he had been so busy with his own life and problems, he hadn't realized how deep his love for her had grown. He loved her desperately. All along he had known she didn't want to leave Duluth, and he had tried to be satisfied with weekends, but now the weekends were gone and he wanted her permanently. After their upsetting conversation, he had wanted to get on a plane and fly straight to Duluth to tell her how much he loved her, but he couldn't.

He had tried to keep Brian from going to Minnesota, but Brian had wanted to be best man for one of his oldest friends. Brian had promised to be careful, and as long as he was going to be there for the wedding, Mike had asked him to see Savannah and give her a plane ticket to come to New Mexico.

Mike stood up abruptly, his chair scraping on the floor. He jammed his hands into his pockets and paced the kitchen restlessly. It had to be another man, he thought with despair. There couldn't be any other reason for her actions.

Savannah and another man. But why hadn't she just admitted it? From the moment she had threatened him with an ax, she had been forthright and honest with him. So why wasn't she being honest now?

He rubbed the back of his neck distractedly. *Why?* And why had he been so blind to his own feelings for her? He had come alive again with her, and he had been so swamped with worry over the trial and moving that he hadn't realized how badly he needed and loved her, until it was too late.

"Dammit," he muttered. It couldn't be too late! And if she wanted to break off their relationship because she was afraid their growing love would take her from Duluth, they would just face it and try to work things out.

He opened the phone book, and as he thumbed through the pages he snapped, "Mumps, my boo-diddly!" Then he snatched up the phone and called the airport.

Savannah readjusted the blanket on her lap and lowered her knitting to look outside at the first snow of the year. It fell on red maple leaves and yellow mums, big flakes swirling and drifting down. The windows were beginning to frost, reminding Savannah of Christmastime. Christmas, New Year's, "Auld Lang Syne." Snow tumbled in slow-moving streams, mesmerizing. It would cover the ground and then melt, and then spring would come. And her baby would be born. . . .

Savannah wore a blue robe and had tied a blue ribbon around her head to hold her hair away from her face. Pete was staying with her, but had gone out to get groceries. Savannah sighed, feeling a rush of love for her family, who had pitched in to help in every way imaginable.

She hadn't so much as dusted a table since that fateful day at the hospital. Members of her family took turns running errands, staying with her, taking her to see Dr. Borden. They did anything and everything that needed to be done.

It had been a week since Brian had called. The moment her thoughts switched to Mike, she picked up her knitting and resumed her work on the pink, white, and blue baby blanket.

She was bent over her knitting and didn't see the figure striding determinedly up the walk. The first she knew of his presence was when the doorbell rang.

Startled, she slowly got to her feet and straightened her robe. She glanced out the front window and saw a black car parked at the curb.

"Who is it?" she called through the door.

"It's Mike, Savannah," a deep voice replied, and her heart thudded violently against her ribs.

She looked around wildly, as if she could find some solution or help close at hand. Her gaze met her reflection in the hall mirror, and she gasped. For a moment she had forgotten her rounded stomach, her robe, her lack of makeup, and her uncombed hair. She ran her fingers through it distractedly.

"Savannah?" he called.

"I have the mumps."

"I had mumps when I was a kid," he shouted, his voice loud enough for the neighborhood to hear.

You would have! she thought. She bit her lip in uncertainty. "You might be able to get them again!"

"No, I won't, but I might get frostbite!"

"Oh." She didn't want to see him, but she couldn't leave him standing on the steps in a snowstorm. "Mike," she yelled. "I really can't see you now."

"Savannah, open the door or I'll kick it down!"

Her eyes widened, and she stared at the door, almost expecting it to splinter before her eyes. Somehow she had the feeling he wasn't making an idle threat.

Reluctantly she turned the knob and opened the door while her heart began a hammer roll.

Eleven

The sight of Mike standing on her porch, snow-flakes tumbling around him and melting on his shoulders, on his broad-brimmed Stetson, on his thick eyelashes, made Savannah's heart slam against her ribs. She had dreamed about him, conjured up images of him in her mind so many times. Now, with snow falling in hypnotic patterns, and utter silence, she had a sense of unreality. A dreamlike quality enveloped them. He was so handsome! Her breathing was constricted, and she felt suspended in time.

They stood looking into each other's eyes for an eternity. Then his gaze flicked down to the neck of her robe and immediately up again. "You're really sick? You actually have mumps?"

She couldn't lie when she stared straight into his probing blue eyes. She shrugged. "Well, not exactly, now that you get right down to it."

"My toes are getting numb."

"I'm sorry!" she exclaimed, unaware of cold or heat or anything except him. He seemed larger, taller, and more broad-shouldered than she had remembered. Was it his actual presence or the heavy coat, wide-brimmed hat, and western boots that made him seem so overwhelming? For a moment, as he stood silhouetted against the white world behind him, he looked like the only solid, secure thing in existence. She wanted to put her hand out and touch him, but in that direction lay disaster, because it was taking all the control she could exert to remain aloof and deal with him. "Come inside," she said politely, knowing there was no way to keep him out.

He stamped his booted feet, and she glanced down the street, hoping she would see Pete returning or one of her relatives arriving. Then Mike was inside, locking the door behind him, and they were alone.

She turned away quickly. "I'm supposed to rest. I have a blanket on the sofa in the living room. Do you mind coming in there?"

"No," he said, and she could detect a puzzled note in his tone. "But I have snow all over my coat and hat."

"You can hang them in the hall closet," she said, unwilling to turn and face him again. She didn't want to take the coat from him and have Mike study her figure while she hung up his things. She barely showed, but her figure had changed. Her waist had thickened, and her stomach was beginning to have a roundness to it. It was early in November now, the start of the fourth month of her pregnancy. She felt a pull on her senses and glanced to her left.

She had forgotten the hall mirror. Mike was staring at her reflection. At her profile. His gaze lowered, drifting down, and, too late, she realized how revealing her reflection was. She had belted the old cotton robe tightly, and it clearly revealed the slight new fullness of her figure.

She felt a blush start at her throat and send scalding waves of heat into her cheeks as he studied the rounded contours of her figure. Then he looked up. Her gaze met his shocked one in the mirror.

"You're pregnant!" he whispered.

She moved then, the spell broken. She hurried to the safety of the couch and pulled the blanket to her chin, huddling beneath it. He followed her and stood only a few yards away, his feet spread slightly apart, his topcoat open, revealing navy slacks and a heavy navy sweater. Locks of hair tumbled onto his forehead as he studied her with a burning look, and she could almost see the quick calculation he was making. Then she saw the full realization in his expression that she was carrying his child.

"Why didn't you tell me?" he asked, and his voice was a whiplash, cutting through her sharply.

She raised her chin, looking at him defiantly. Then suddenly he moved, and all the harshness went out of his expression. He sat down beside her and scooped her into his arms, crushing her to his chest.

"Savannah, I love you and I missed you and I've been in agony. I could wring your beautiful neck for putting me through this hell! And I'm sorry. If you'd just told me . . . I'll get a minister and we can be mar—"

"No," she said flatly, wriggling out of his grasp and scooting back against the sofa. "I won't marry you."

Stunned again, Mike stared at her as shock buffeted him like the cold north wind outside. "Why?" he asked.

Snow had melted on his lashes, and the crystal drops looked like tears. She firmed her lips. "I'm not well, Mike. I have to be very careful, or I'll lose the baby."

He watched her and felt as if his heart were breaking in two. She looked incredibly beautiful. He was reeling from the shock, trying to sort out what had happened and why she was acting so strangely. Was she furious over the pregnancy? "Oh, love, why didn't you let me know? Why, Savannah?"

She looked down at her hand as snowflakes melted and dropped off his coat sleeve, sending sprinkles of cold wetness onto her skin. She tried to scoot away from him, wishing she could avoid him altogether. Yet how marvelous he looked! So solid and safe, and all she had remembered and dreamed about. And now because of his sense of duty and obligation, he would persist in trying to do the right thing and marry her.

"I'm getting wet," she said.

He glanced down, and without a word, stripped off his coat and hat and dumped them on the floor. When he tilted her chin up, she pulled away.

"Mike, if I had wanted to talk about it with you, I would have."

"Look at me, dammit!"

"Don't shout at me!" she snapped back, glaring at him.

"I assumed you went to your doctor for contraceptives."

She shrugged, wishing she could escape his steady, intense watchfulness. He rested his chin on his hand and his elbow on his knee to study her, and she looked down, fiddling with the covers.

"If you were any other woman on earth, I'd say you were madder than hell because you're pregnant, but I don't think that's what's wrong."

"No, it's not. I got pregnant deliberately. I loved you and I wanted your baby." Fiery green eyes snapped up to meet his gaze momentarily.

Stunned, he was silent for a minute. "You've always wanted a baby," he whispered, trying to reason out her actions.

"Will you please stop trying to analyze something that isn't any of your business and leave me be!"

"In a word, no."

Their gazes locked in another silent contest while he tried to put together the jumbled pieces of a puzzle called Savannah. "How many days have you been home from school?"

Her lashes dropped instantly, hiding her eyes from him. "A few."

He knew she was lying to him. She did it poorly, and it only confused him more. And then he remembered the perfectly logical reason that had kept him from trying to get her to make more of a commitment: She loved her family and job and Duluth too much to leave, and she knew he couldn't safely move back to Minnesota. She loved her single life so much, she was willing to be a single parent to keep what she had. He knew how badly she must have wanted a baby for years. She was very much in command of her life, and she had probably decided she could manage a baby just fine on her own. Well, he was in love, and if it meant living where his life was in danger, he would. He rubbed his hand on his knee while he thought about it, and the idea seemed the most reasonable one he could come up with.

"Look at me, will you?"

She shot him another angry glance. "Don't you badger me! I'm sick."

"All I asked you to do was look at me," he said gently, and her lashes fluttered. She raised her chin and glared at him, just as she had done so long ago when she had threatened him with the ax. She looked brave, and as if she were about to face a monstrous task.

"Now, tell me you don't still love me and I'll go back to New Mexico," he said, and he felt as if his lungs had stopped functioning and his heart had quit

beating. He saw her quick intake of breath and a
flicker of something that closely resembled fear in
her eyes, before she looked down at the blanket. His
heart began beating again at a faster rate. He expelled his breath in a rush while hope blossomed
inside him like flowers in a desert.

"For Lord's sake, will you look at me, Savannah?"

"I feel terrible, and you're making me feel worse,"
she said as she lay back, her eyes closed.

"And you still love me," he said softly, leaning
forward to brush her lips with his. He hurt badly, he
wanted her so. With her fuller figure, pale face, and
tousled hair tied in a simple ribbon, she had never
looked more beautiful to him. His lips touched hers
so lightly, tasting a sweetness that made him hard
with desire.

Instantly her eyes opened, and she drew back,
twisting her head. "Mike! Don't!"

This time she sounded sincere, and faced him
with a totally honest expression on her face. "Dr.
Borden said no sex. *No sex.*"

"All I did—"

"—was too much," she whispered, and something
vibrated all through his insides, as if he were coming apart.

"Please," she said. "We've been separated for a
long time. You can't kiss me."

He leaned back suddenly, afraid of hurting her,
while he digested this fact. No sex. Brian had been
up a week ago, and Savannah had claimed illness
then. No sex meant something serious. "How long
has it been since you last taught?"

"A while," she said, looking away, a sign that was
becoming ridiculously obvious to Mike that meant
she didn't want to be truthful.

"If you weren't so damned sick and so damned

sweet, I'd shake you! Did you know that you can't look me in the eye and lie?"

He received a glare from her for that one! "Now, how long have you been home from work?"

"Several weeks," she said tiredly, and cold fear gripped him.

"What's wrong?" he asked quietly.

"Mike, you're exhausting me. This won't get us anywhere. I don't want to discuss it with you and—"

"Okay, put your head back, honey." He stood up and jammed his hands into his pockets as he studied her. She lay back on the pillows with her eyes closed, but he had a suspicion they weren't fully closed, and that she was watching him.

"I'll just talk to you, since you won't talk to me," he said cheerfully, rubbing the nape of his neck. "You love me . . . you can't deny it." She squeezed her eyes shut, and his hopes rose another fraction. "You're going to have our baby. You got pregnant deliberately. Anyway, it's awfully late now for an abortion."

Again he got a swift, angry look from her. "I wouldn't have an abortion!" she exclaimed with so much indignation that he felt his heart swell.

"Of course you wouldn't," he said tenderly, and moved back a step, clenching his fists to keep from touching her. "You're not teaching. When are you going back?"

"I don't know."

"Savannah, do you know you are an absolutely lousy liar?"

He received another wide-eyed, startled glance, and he suffered a rush of impatience over having to drag everything out of her. "You must have quit your teaching job."

"Yes, I did!" she snapped, and this time there was unmistakable fire in her eyes.

He tried to control his surprise and shock, because he realized she must have had a terribly bad time, to have had to quit teaching and be home in bed all the time. He couldn't bear to think about it, and, unable to control what he was feeling, he moved back to the sofa and sat down beside her. "Honey," he said gently, taking her hand, "why didn't you let me know?"

She turned away, her voice only a whisper as she tried to pull her hand from his. "Mike, don't make this so hard on both of us."

"I know what's wrong, Savannah." When she faced him again, he said, "You don't want to leave your family and life here, and you know I can't move back."

To his amazement he saw emotions flicker over her expressive features, and he would have sworn the first had been surprise. His deduction about her actions must have been wrong! All this time he had wrestled with a dilemma that might not have existed. Suddenly he was more confused than ever. *Why?*

"This is a dead-end situation," she said. "I don't want to marry you. Period."

"Why not? I have a claim on this baby, you know. And *her* mother loves me."

"It's a boy, and you don't have any claim on us, Mike," Savannah said flatly, and he felt another jolt. She was angry and bitter, and for the life of him he couldn't think why. He saw that her brow was dotted with perspiration, and he realized she might not be in any shape for an emotional upheaval.

He smoothed the collar of her robe, trying to keep his touch as impersonal as possible, but her eyes darkened and he took his hands away. "Okay. Let's talk about the weather or something, so I don't tire you."

"Thank you," she said, and closed her eyes, putting her head back on the pillow.

He wanted her so badly, he wouldn't have believed it possible. And he couldn't even kiss her on the cheek. For a fleeting instant he silently cursed himself for being such a fool when he had moved to Santa Fe, by not asking Savannah to marry him then. He had thought they had all the time in the world to let their love grow into a permanent commitment, but it was too late for that now.

They sat quietly for over ten minutes. Savannah didn't move or open her eyes, and he kept glancing at her. He saw the dark circles under her eyes, the paleness of her skin.

"Can you have a normal pregnancy and delivery?"

"I hope so."

"Can you tell me what the doctor told you?"

"I have recurrent uterine bleeding," she said quietly, and explained it to him with her eyes closed. She sounded exhausted, and he knew he should get up and leave her alone, but he couldn't. The problem scared him, and he stared at her, wanting to do everything in his power to help her and feeling the wildest frustration because she wouldn't let him do a thing. Or share any part of the time with him.

"You want . . ." He hated the raspy note in his voice, but he couldn't control it. "You want me to go back to New Mexico and leave you alone through this?"

She opened her eyes and looked directly into his. "Yes, please. I do want that."

All the pain he had felt before intensified, because he knew she was telling the truth this time. His words were only a whisper. "Is it because you think I'm in danger here?"

"No," she said flatly, and shook her head.

"That isn't why you won't marry me—because you

don't want to leave your family and you're afraid for me to live here again?"

"No, Mike, it's not," she said quietly, her gaze never wavering. He stood up and walked over to the window, seeing the snow through a wavering haze of tears that he fought to keep under control. His throat burned, and he couldn't understand what had happened, what he had done or hadn't done, or why she wanted him to go, when she still loved him and carried his child.

When he got his emotions under control he turned around. His movement was abrupt; she obviously hadn't been expecting it, and he caught her staring at him.

She didn't look away quickly enough, and he saw the longing that was plainly visible in her eyes. He felt as if an invisible fist had slammed into his middle. He drew a sharp breath. She closed her eyes again, shutting him out of her world.

He crossed the room to her and sat down on the sofa. "Savannah."

She looked at him warily, as if he were someone she feared.

"Can I untie your robe and just look at you? Can I put my hand where the baby is just once?"

He could have sworn her eyes filled with tears before she nodded and closed them and turned her face away. He wanted to yank her chin up and see if she was on the verge of crying, but he didn't. Very carefully he untied her robe and opened it, then placed his hand on her abdomen.

"Can you feel the baby move yet?"

"No, but Dr. Borden said I will any time now."

He wanted to stroke her cheek, to kiss her lightly, to do anything to care for her. Suddenly a key turned in the back door, and he heard the sound of stomping feet as a deep male voice called, "Savannah, I'm here!"

Mike's head jerked up, his nostrils flaring, and for a wild instant he had a dreadful feeling in the pit of his stomach. He blinked, closing her robe as he looked down at her.

Savannah blushed, her cheeks becoming as pink as roses, and she sat up straight, pulling the blanket back up over her.

"We're in here," she called. "It's my brother, with groceries," she whispered quickly to Mike.

His immediate reaction of relief was so intense, it must have shown, because she frowned. His next reaction was anger and regret that her brother was allowed to do the things he should have been doing.

Mike stood up and moved around the sofa toward the kitchen as Pete entered the living room. Taller than Savannah, Pete had the same silky blond hair, and it showed from beneath a bright red stocking cap, which he had pushed to the back of his head.

"Man alive, it's cold! I brought you a scrumptious—" Pete bit off his words when he saw Mike.

"Oh, sorry!" he went on after a moment. "I saw the car at the curb, but I thought it was the neighbor's." He extended his hand to take Mike's. "Glad to see you," he said in a peculiar tone of voice, and Mike wondered whether Pete actually wanted to slug him or if he was sincerely welcoming him.

"I'm glad to see you," Mike said. "I came to talk to Savannah."

"I didn't mean to intrude. I'll be running along."

"Don't go, Pete," Savannah said quickly. "Mike is leaving, and there are some things I need your help with."

Pete looked questioningly at Mike, and suddenly Mike had a hunch that whatever Savannah held against him, her family didn't.

"Let me help you with the groceries," Mike said firmly, taking Pete's arm and propelling him into the kitchen.

Savannah gritted her teeth. Damn Mike and his aggressive tendencies! she thought. Pete would probably tell him in great detail every single thing he knew. She ran her hand across her forehead. She couldn't cope with Mike. The past hour had exhausted her. It seemed as if it had been days, instead of just a little more than sixty minutes. And in another few minutes Mike would be gone.

She closed her eyes and slipped down on the sofa, hoping she could go to sleep. If she didn't, she would pretend she had, and maybe Mike would go without further confrontations. An image of him came to mind. He had run his fingers through his hair until the thick curls were a tangle. And the lightest, briefest touch of his lips on hers had frightened her, because her reaction had been so intense.

She shut that moment out of her thoughts, trying to think about something safer. What was he doing with Pete? She lay still, straining to hear and not catching a sound from the kitchen, until the back door slammed and all was silent. Curious, she raised herself up to look into the kitchen, but didn't see a sign of anyone. She sank back down on the cushions, feeling exhausted.

When Savannah opened her eyes later, she was relieved to find that she had dozed. She twisted around, to see Mike seated beside her, holding her hand and watching her.

"You've been asleep. Feel better?"

"Yes." She glanced around the empty room. Snow was still tumbling outside the windows. "Where's Pete?"

"I told him to go on to work, that I'd do whatever tasks you have."

"Is Mom here yet?"

"I sent her home."

"You just have to take charge of everything," she said accusingly, studying him. He looked far more relaxed, and she realized he had talked with her mother and her brother. "I won't marry you."

He pursed his lips, and she suspected she should have rested longer. He was laughing at her! She squinted, then stared at him.

He faced her calmly, not a flicker of an expression on his face, although a muscle worked in his jaw.

"Okay, Savannah," he said cheerfully, tucking the blanket around her shoulders. "But my flight home has been canceled, and since you let me stay here weeks before, I thought you might agree to let me spend the night."

"That's fine, Mike, but my family—"

"I've talked to them, and thanks for saying it's fine. Pete and Maggie told me what needs to be done. I have a load of laundry drying now, a roast in the oven, and I'm going out to shovel the walk if you don't need me for a few minutes."

She could smell a rat, and she knew where to lay the blame—squarely on her family. Pete and her mom had probably told Mike everything Savannah had told them. She stared at him for several long minutes.

"Well?" he asked.

"We might as well get it said and out in the open now. You want to marry me because of the baby, and I will not marry you for that reason!"

"I understand," he said politely. "Anything you want before I go out to shovel?"

"You don't have to shovel my walk! My brother—"

"—was so relieved, he couldn't wait to get in his car and go. Not that he doesn't love you, but he has his own walk and drive to shovel."

"One night."

"Sure, Savannah."

"Why aren't you arguing?"

"You want me to argue with you?" he asked mildly.

"There's something suspicious about your agree-ableness. Are you going to go back to Santa Fe and leave me alone?"

He stood up and winked at her. "Hon, whatever makes you happy. I know I wore you out this morning, and I promise I won't do that again."

She had a feeling down to the marrow of her bones that Mike was up to something. All the worry had gone out of his voice, and he sounded as happy as a cream-filled cat.

"You won't ask me to marry you again?"

"Oh, I don't know," he replied with uncustomary breeziness. "I hate to promise that, when who knows what may happen a couple of years from now, when our baby is toddling around?"

Our baby. In spite of the tension and strain of the day, the words sent a thrill through her. She ruffled the blanket. "Mike, you're just stalling," she said, but her voice had changed. *Our baby.*

"No, I'm not. I promise you that," he said, and he sounded as if he meant it. He pulled on a down-filled jacket, and she stared at it.

"That isn't the coat you were wearing when you came."

"Nope. When I learned all flights were canceled, I asked Pete to go to the nearest mall and get me a few things. A robe, slippers, toothbrush, jacket. I'll be back in a minute."

He left, whistling as he went, and she knew something had changed totally. Something in Mike's mind. Hers was still the same. She was adamant about not marrying him simply because she was pregnant.

She raised herself up to look at Mike as he walked

through the kitchen. At the door he turned, caught her watching him, and winked. She sank back down, her thoughts in a quandary. She wasn't convinced Mike would spend the night, get on a plane tomorrow, and never look back.

Maybe her family had told him of her feelings, but she didn't think he would be so obviously happy to be free from the responsibility of marriage and fatherhood. Not at all. Mike was one to shoulder responsibility as surely as he was standing on her front walk shoveling snow! She bit her lip and watched him work, and for the first time she let herself relish every second of looking at him. It was sheer heaven to have him in Duluth! She wanted to feel his arms around her, to cling to him and just have him hold her and stay with her.

But she absolutely refused to let him marry her out of a sense of responsibility. She would never do that! She had to have his love above all else.

Mike was working swiftly and with apparent ease, the wind tossing his hair. Savannah went into the bathroom and began to make some repairs on her hair, brushing it out and discarding the ribbon. She dressed in a full-fitting blue wool jumper with a pale blue sweater beneath it. Running her hand over her stomach, she remembered when Mike had placed his hand there, and a tingly excitement began to grow in her. Mike was here, and nothing seemed as bad as before.

She heard the back door slam, then feet stamping, and a clatter from Mike.

"I'm home, honey," he called.

"I'm in my room. I'll be right there," she called back, his words causing her to smile. In seconds he filled the doorway. His cheeks were ruddy, his hair tousled, and he was handsome enough to make her melt into a boneless heap.

"Don't you look pretty!" he said softly, taking in her appearance.

"*Pretty* is hardly the right word! I'm getting big," she said, glancing at herself in the mirror.

She saw his reflection as he moved to stand behind her.

Mike placed his hands on her shoulders. "You look beautiful. Absolutely beautiful. And I love you." He said the words quietly, but they seemed to pound in her ears with a roaring echo.

"I want you to marry me."

"Mike, I can't stand here and argue. I'm supposed to stay in bed, but I got up to get dressed, since I have company."

"Who?"

"You!"

"You shouldn't have dressed for me. Come back to the sofa."

She settled herself comfortably on the sofa and listened to Mike talk about Santa Fe, his business, and the New Mexico weather. He left to get the laundry, and brought it with him, folding it while he talked. She watched him, wondering how many times in his life he had folded laundry.

"I've decided to get started in my own business sooner," he said. "I'm going to give notice in April."

"You are?"

"Yep. I'll take a little time off, then settle down to my very own business."

"That's nice," she said, thinking it was an odd coincidence that he had decided to make the change at about the same time their baby would be born.

"Getting hungry?" he asked.

"A little."

"Dinner's coming right up." He picked up the basket of folded laundry and left the room. In minutes she could hear him puttering in the kitchen, and in less than an hour he was serving steaming slices of roast. He brought their meal in on a tray, so she could stay on the sofa.

They talked until nine. The fire burned low, snow still pelted the windows, and it was sheer heaven to have him with her. He sat on the floor beside the sofa, talking to her, stroking her arm, touching her constantly with light, brotherly touches. They shouldn't have had a melting effect on her, but each one did, no matter how casual it was. Without thinking about what she was doing she wound her fingers in his hair, until he turned his head and kissed her palm.

She sucked in her breath. She had let down her guard completely, and without warning, hot tears stung her eyes as all her iron control slipped away. She turned her head quickly, wiping her eyes.

"Hey, Savannah, honey," he said tenderly. He sat beside her on the sofa, placing his hands on both sides of her face.

"Are you crying?"

"No!" she whispered, trying to regain her control and put up the barriers again. "I can't cry, Mike, so let's change the subject. I'm afraid if I cry it'll do something to my health." She knew she was talking too fast and avoiding his eyes, but couldn't help herself. "I won't cry until April, after the baby comes. I always promise myself—"

"You won't cry until *April?*"

The shock in his voice brought her up short. She looked up to see him watching her with such a pained expression that she wanted to put her arms around him and reassure him.

"Mike, talk about something else. Movies, something. Please. When you're not here I think of schoolwork or babies' names or the nursery. You see, when I start talking about Jeff, I can calm myself."

"Oh, Lord, Savannah!" he said, and he sounded agonized. He put his arms around her and buried his face against her neck.

"Mike, don't make me cry. I just can't."

"What if Jeff's a girl?" he asked in a shaky voice.

"Then we'll name her Michelle," she said, without realizing she had used the plural pronoun instead of the singular. They talked about babies and nursery colors, and both of them seemed to calm down and get a tighter grip on their emotions. Mike sat up, fiddling with a lock of her hair while they talked.

When she couldn't stifle a yawn, he stood, picking her up easily in spite of her protests. "Mike, I'm so heavy."

"Yeah, sure. You've gained all of, what, four pounds?"

She laughed and put her arms around his neck. "Not too much yet. Ginny says it will come faster from now on."

"She should know." He set her on her feet beside her bed. "Need any more help?"

"No, thank you," she said softly, wanting him in bed with her, wanting his arms to stay around her. She turned quickly, feeling forlorn.

" 'Night, honey."

" 'Night, Mike. Thanks for all your help."

"Sure thing."

After he closed the door she sank down on the bed. She stared at the door, listening to Mike moving around the house. How wonderful it was to have him there! For an instant she wondered what would happen if she married him, even if it wasn't what he really wanted. He loved her, to a degree. Would he really miss his freedom?

She shook her head. Thoughts like that could bring disaster. Total disaster. Mike had told her he didn't want to marry, and she wouldn't force him into it because she had wanted his baby!

She shifted her thoughts to the nursery, the familiar things that usually soothed her, but tonight thoughts of Mike kept getting in the way.

The next day the snow stopped. Mike kissed her good-bye, told her gruffly to take care of herself and call him if she wanted him, and he left.

And she was bereft. She sat on the sofa feeling imprisoned, trying to listen politely to Ginny's chatter, to get her mind off Mike, but she hurt all over.

And she didn't feel any better as the rest of the week passed. Mike called each night, and they talked for about an hour about inconsequential things, but the calls only made her miss him more. She vaguely noticed that her family, while still solicitous, didn't seem half as concerned about her.

On the next cold, clear Friday morning in November, Savannah was alone. She just happened to look out the window to see a black car park at the curb. Mike emerged from the car, his arms loaded with boxes. Her heart jumped with anticipation and dread. She remembered when they had last parted, and wondered if he would continue to fly up to Duluth on weekends during her pregnancy. Her family had stopped urging her to change her mind about marrying him. They had stopped urging her to do anything except rest.

She went to the door, and before she opened it, she paused to look at herself in the hall mirror. She wished Mike would let her know when he was coming!

Her hair was tied in a ribbon again, she was in the same old bathrobe, and she wasn't wearing a speck of makeup.

She opened the door, to find him stamping snow off his feet.

"Hello, there."

"Mike, why don't you at least call from the airport? I would brush my hair and put on some makeup."

His eyes sparkled as he came inside along with a rush of cold air. He looked big, male, handsome, *gorgeous!* He kissed her lightly on the cheek. "Go get back on the sofa. I brought you a present."

He sounded happy as a lark, and her suspicions began to rise.

She sank down, pulled a blanket over her lap, and waited, listening to him whistle as he hung up his coat. He looked incredibly handsome. His skin was tanned and his hair tumbled over his forehead. He wore a dark suit and white shirt that looked as if they had been tailored just for him.

"Happy today!" he said cheerfully, and placed a huge box beside her.

She looked at him questioningly before she began to untie the pink ribbon. She tore away the wrapping paper and pushed open the box, to lift out a white satin dress. It had yards and yards of material gathered high, beneath the bustline, and long sleeves and a high neck. A wedding dress.

"Mike, I can't take this," she said stonily.

"Oh, but you can and will, because you love me and I love you and you have a damnfool notion I don't want to be married, when I want that more than anything on earth!"

It was finally out in the open. "I don't believe you," she said firmly and quietly, and folded the dress back into the box.

"Look at me." He caught her hands, and she looked into eyes the color of a stormy ocean. "Do I seem like a man who's committing an act of charity? Do I look reluctant?"

It was becoming increasingly difficult for her to breathe, and a bubbly feeling began to tickle her senses. "If you had wanted to marry, you would have asked me *before* you found out I was pregnant. You're a mature man with a strong sense of duty."

"Bull," he said quietly, but she heard the familiar note of steel in his voice.

"You won't convince me otherwise, because until you found out I was pregnant, marriage, commitment, or anything close to it never entered a conversation we had."

"That's because I was recuperating from the trauma I had gone through and didn't have the sense to stop and look at what I felt and what was happening to me. And when I did, I didn't think you'd leave Duluth. I kept hoping that with time, your visits to Santa Fe, and the separation, I might win you away from your life here," he said solemnly, and her heart began to skip beats, becoming as erratic as her breathing. She looked searchingly into his eyes. He sounded convincing. But she could remember only too well . . .

"Mike, this won't work if we don't *love*. I've been through that before. I mean deeply and truly love each other."

"Do you think I would do all this if I didn't really love you?" He framed her face with his hands. "I want you and our baby beyond anything I've ever wanted before, because I realize how close I came to losing you both."

Her throat constricted tightly. She was scared to let go of her fears and trust him, because if he didn't mean what he said, it would be worse later.

"Savannah," he whispered, and leaned forward to kiss her lightly, sweetly on the lips. "I love you. And

I've loved you for a long time now. You've given me back some youth and a new life and love and a baby . . . our baby. How can you doubt me?"

He pulled back to look into her eyes.

She took a deep breath. "You said so positively you didn't want to marry again because you never wanted to be hurt that badly." She could barely whisper the words, but she had to be sure.

"I know what the hell I said, but if you'll recall, I wasn't living a normal life at the time. And I wasn't head over heels in love with you that first night on the boat."

He smoothed her hair away from her face. "This isn't fair. I can't slug you again and carry you off to New Mexico with me, or kiss you into saying yes."

She tried to smile, but she couldn't. Too much was at stake.

"Marry me, Savannah."

She sat there trying to decide, wanting to cry with joy, wanting to tell him yes, but remembering the breakup of her marriage and the agony and pain and disappointment she had felt.

Mike wrapped his arms around her and nestled his head against her shoulder to whisper in her ear. "Take a chance that I'm telling the truth. I love you and our baby, and I'll move back to Duluth and camp on your doorstep if you don't consent."

"Mike, don't threaten or push. Maybe we should wait until after—"

"Hell, no!" he snapped, sitting up. "Dammit, do you know what this is doing to me! I just went through one trauma, and now I have to go through another one that's worse! I love you!"

His voice was hoarse and his eyes were red, and Savannah drew a sharp breath as she stared at him.

"Oh, Mike!" She blinked, unable to believe that he cared enough to lose control of his emotions. Suddenly she let go, and it was as if a dam had broken inside her. "I've wanted you so badly." She felt her tears come, and she threw herself against him.

Strong arms enveloped her and crushed her to him as she sobbed against his chest.

"Savannah, dammit, stop crying! You promised you'd wait until April to cry."

She laughed through her tears and wiped her eyes as she looked up at him.

"This is your last chance, Mike. Are you sure?"

"Absolutely," he said tenderly, wiping her wet cheeks with his thumbs. "I want you and Michelle with all my heart and soul."

She clung to him, squeezing him tightly as she turned her head to kiss his throat. "It's Jeff. Not Michelle."

Mike chuckled. "I have an ambulance waiting, a plane waiting, and another plane chartered for your family. We can fly to Santa Fe for our wedding. It will be very, very simple. I found an excellent doctor there, but if you want to stay right here, that's the way we'll do it. You decide what you want, Savannah."

She looked at him, unable to think about anything except marrying him. "I don't know," she said vaguely, and a crooked smile tugged at the corner of his mouth.

"You don't mind leaving Dr. Borden?"

She tried to think about something besides Mike, but it was difficult.

"Savannah, Dr. Borden!" Mike said with amusement.

She would miss Dr. Borden, but when she had first discovered her pregnancy and hoped Mike would ask her to marry him, she had been fully prepared to move to Santa Fe. She thought about the baby and what would be best for him. "You're sure you have a good doctor?"

"Honey, he's been highly recommended, but the choice has to be entirely yours."

"Dr. Borden said I had to be careful during my pregnancy, but I should have a normal delivery."

"You want to talk it over with him? He said to give him a call."

"You talked to everyone. Sort of high-handed—"

"You forced me into it," he said mildly. He picked up the phone and handed her the receiver, then punched the numbers. He left the room while she talked with Dr. Borden, then returned before she was through. He sat beside her, and placed the phone on the floor when she had finished.

"He says to go, that I should get along fine and it will make our lives less complicated."

"You're sure?"

She nodded.

Mike smiled at her, his blue eyes filled with love. "You don't know what I went through," he said tenderly, "and I knew it was because of my own foolishness in not marrying you the moment I moved to New Mexico. And for a time I underestimated my own charm. I was sure you wouldn't want to leave your family and your life here."

"It doesn't matter now," she whispered, locking her arms around his neck.

"I love you, sweetie, and Michelle."

"Jeff. Jeff with blue eyes."

He shook his head. "Lord, you're stubborn." He smiled at her, and she felt as if she were glowing with happiness. Tears of joy threatened, and as she blinked rapidly, he frowned.

"Hey! You can't cry until April!" He leaned down to nuzzle her neck. She wriggled away and smiled at him.

"You can't do that until April either."

They gazed at each other with rapt love. "You

won't really be disappointed if it's a boy, will you?" she asked softly.

"What do you think?" He pulled her onto his lap and held her close to his heart, smoothing her hair. "This baby is ours—that's all that matters."

Feeling in complete agreement with him, Savannah tightened her arms around Mike's neck. "I can't wait until April for a number of reasons—and none of them is so I can cry!"

He chuckled and kissed her throat lightly, while she closed her eyes and dreamed of the future.

THE EDITOR'S CORNER

Last month I briefly told you the good news that The Delaney Dynasty lives on! Next month you'll get a sneak preview of the second trio of Delaney books, **THE DELANEYS OF KILLAROO,** in a Free Sampler you'll see everywhere! It's part of a promotion that is unique in publishing history and is being done jointly by LOVESWEPT and Clairol®. In the late fall last year, a creative and effervescent young woman representing Clairol, Inc., came to see us at Bantam. Their market research had identified the "perfect user" of a new hair product they were developing as the same woman who reads LOVESWEPT romances! You, my friends out there, were described as intelligent, clever, fun loving, optimistic, romantic women who cared about and tried to make a contribution to family, friends, community, and country. Sounds right to me, I said. The new product from Clairol®—PAZAZZ® SHEER COLORWASH—is a continuation of the PAZAZZ® line of temporary (and, I must add, fun) coloring gels, mousses, and color wands. But what truly amazed me was that one of the colors they had "invented"—*Sheer Plum* —had just been "invented" by Fayrene Preston for her heroine Sydney in **THE DELANEYS OF KILLAROO.** Further, while Iris Johansen's and Kay Hooper's heroines weren't described in the precise terms of the new Clairol® colors, they were so close that one had to begin to believe that our two companies were fated to get together with **THE DELANEYS OF KILLAROO** and **PAZAZZ® SHEER COLORWASH.** So we decided to do a promotion featuring a Sampler of the new books about the Australian branch of the Delaney family, whose heroines had Sheer Colorwash hair colors. And in each Sampler Clairol® gives you a Beauty Bonus full of tips on hair beauty and styling using the new products. Next month at health and beauty aid sections of stores and at cosmetic counters you will find the Free Sampler. You'll also find the Free Samplers when you go to your local bookselling outlet. In all, more than three-quarters of a million copies of these Samplers will be given away during a six-week period. Then, when **THE DELANEYS OF KILLAROO** books are published in August, the first 200,000 copies of each title will carry a special money-saving coupon from Clairol® so that you—you "perfect users" you!—can try

(continued)

PAZAZZ® SHEER COLORWASH at a lower price. I hope you'll enjoy this promotion since you are its special focus. Lots of other women who may never have heard of LOVE-SWEPT romances will learn about them, too, as all of us learn for the first time about a brand-new way to put more PAZAZZ® into our lives with color highlights ranging from subtle to dramatic ... from the glints of gold in Sheer Cinnamon or Amber to the glow of a fine wine in Sheer Plum or Burgundy. We on the LOVESWEPT staff have been treated by Clairol® to samples of all these products ... and if you could see us now! We, in turn, treated the Clairol® ladies to the Delaney books and other LOVESWEPTs, and they loved them! We've had so much fun with this promotion, and we hope you, too, will enjoy this first-ever promotion with you in mind.

Now for a few words about the delightful LOVESWEPTs in store for you next month.

We are so pleased to introduce a wonderful new talent, Glenna McReynolds, making her debut as a published author with **SCOUT'S HONOR**, LOVESWEPT #198. In this charming love story Mitch Summers, a wonderfully masterful and yet vulnerable man, follows stunningly beautiful Anna Lange from San Francisco to the Bahamas to ask her a simple favor: would she turn her gambling skills on a cheating cardsharp and win back the land his brother lost in a crooked poker game? After a disastrous experience with a fortune hunter, Anna holds all men at arm's length, but she cannot resist Mitch's boyish charm ... or his passionate kisses. With the glamour of high stakes poker and with the heart-warming emotion of sensuous romance, this is a fabulous first love story from Glenna McReynolds.

Prepare to be glued to your chair, unable to put down **ALLURE**, LOVESWEPT #199, by Fayrene Preston. Breath-takingly passionate and emotional, **ALLURE** is the love story of Rick O'Neill and Chandra Stuart, star-crossed lovers who meet once more after years apart. Only Rick can't remember very much about Chandra, and she has never been able to forget a single thing about him! Then, haunted by a scent that brings along with it a powerful memory, Rick begins to unravel the mystery of the past ... and blaze a trail toward a future with the woman he loves. An enthralling, powerful romance.

(continued)

We are delighted to announce that Joan Bramsch—author of such wonderful, beloved LOVESWEPTs as **THE SOPHISTI-CATED MOUNTAIN GAL** and **THE STALLION MAN**—has the distinction of being the author of our two-hundredth LOVESWEPT, **WITH NO RESERVATIONS**! Hotel executive Ann Waverly is understandably intrigued by Jeffrey Madison. The first time she meets him he looks like something the cat dragged in; the second time, he's wearing only a sheet! Jeffrey is powerfully attracted to Ann, but his suspicious actions make her wary of him and the potent effect he has on her senses. Actually, both Ann and Jeffrey have their secrets, and you'll be kept on the edge of your seat as Joan skillfully weaves this tale of humor and deep love.

Linda Cajio gives us another lighthearted and touching romance with **RESCUING DIANA**, LOVESWEPT #201. At a reception Adam Roberts is captivated by Diana Windsor—nicknamed Princess Di—an endearingly innocent and shy creator of computer games. Diana is equally enchanted by Adam—he's her knight in shining armor come to life. But neither Adam nor Diana expected he would *really* have to rescue this princess from all sorts of modern-day dragons. As you follow Adam and Diana from one delightful escapade to another, you'll fall as much in love with them as they do with each other.

Enjoy!
Warm regards,

Carolyn Nichols

Carolyn Nichols
 Editor
LOVESWEPT
Bantam Books, Inc.
666 Fifth Avenue
New York, NY 10103

The first Delaney trilogy

Heirs to a great dynasty, the Delaney brothers were united by blood, united by devotion to their rugged land . . . and known far and wide as

THE SHAMROCK TRINITY

Bantam's bestselling LOVESWEPT romance line built its reputation on quality and innovation. Now, a remarkable and unique event in romance publishing comes from the same source: THE SHAMROCK TRINITY, three daringly original novels written by three of the most successful women's romance writers today. Kay Hooper, Iris Johansen, and Fayrene Preston have created a trio of books that are dynamite love stories bursting with strong, fascinating male and female characters, deeply sensual love scenes, the humor for which LOVESWEPT is famous, and a deliciously fresh approach to romance writing.

THE SHAMROCK TRINITY—Burke, York, and Rafe: Powerful men . . . rakes and charmers . . . they needed only love to make their lives complete.

☐ *RAFE, THE MAVERICK by Kay Hooper*

Rafe Delaney was a heartbreaker whose ebony eyes held laughing devils and whose lilting voice could charm any lady—or any horse—until a stallion named Diablo left him in the dust. It took Maggie O'Riley to work her magic on the impossible horse . . . and on his bold owner. Maggie's grace and strength made Rafe yearn to share the raw beauty of his land with her, to teach her the exquisite pleasure of yielding to the heat inside her. Maggie was stirred by Rafe's passion, but would his reputation and her ambition keep their kindred spirits apart? (21846 • $2.75)

LOVESWEPT

☐ *YORK, THE RENEGADE* by Iris Johansen

Some men were made to fight dragons, Sierra Smith thought when she first met York Delaney. The rebel brother had roamed the world for years before calling the rough mining town of Hell's Bluff home. Now, the spirited young woman who'd penetrated this renegade's paradise had awakened a savage and tender possessiveness in York: something he never expected to find in himself. Sierra had known loneliness and isolation too—enough to realize that York's restlessness had only to do with finding a place to belong. Could she convince him that love was such a place, that the refuge he'd always sought was in her arms?

(21847 • $2.75)

☐ *BURKE, THE KINGPIN* by Fayrene Preston

Cara Winston appeared as a fantasy, racing on horseback to catch the day's last light—her silver hair glistening, her dress the color of the Arizona sunset . . . and Burke Delaney wanted her. She was on his horse, on his land: she would have to belong to him too. But Cara was quicksilver, impossible to hold, a wild creature whose scent was midnight flowers and sweet grass. Burke had always taken what he wanted, by willing it or fighting for it; Cara cherished her freedom and refused to believe his love would last. Could he make her see he'd captured her to have and hold forever?

(21848 • $2.75)